Hide and Seek

Robin Scott-Elliot

Published in the UK by Everything with Words Limited
Fifth Floor, 30–31 Furnival Street, London, EC4A 1JQ

www.everythingwithwords.com

Text copyright © Robin Scott-Elliot 2021
Cover and illustrations © Holly Ovenden 2021

Robin Scott-Elliot has asserted his right under the Copyright,
Design and Patents Act 1988 to be identified
as the author of this work.

A catalogue record of this book is available
from the British Library.

ISBN 978-1-911427-24-7

Printed and bound in Great Britain by
CPI Group (UK) Ltd, Croydon CR0 4YY

For Iona

Chapter 1

It was cool in the wardrobe. Everywhere else in the apartment was boiling, so brain boiling you wanted to climb into the ice box and pull the lid over your head. Amélie Dreyfus didn't mind being shut in. It's why she was so good at cache-cache, or hide-and-seek as Maman called it when she forgot she wasn't supposed to be British anymore.

Amélie pulled Maman's fur coat towards her and buried her head in it. It tickled her face, as softly as Maman's touch and smelt of her too, her perfume, an aroma of lemons and happiness. Her mother was the best-dressed person in the block, even the whole arrondissement. People expected Amélie to be like her, but she wasn't. It was her brother Paul who followed in Maman's footsteps.

Paulie stood out because he was a Zazou. Amélie didn't absolutely know what that meant apart from he dressed differently to most boys. Maman said in the olden days they would have been called dandies. But they were Zazous and wore big stripy jackets and dark glasses and carried rolled-up umbrellas even at the height of summer. Paulie liked American music and was always humming a tune; bebop he called it.

He was 19, six years older than Amélie, and didn't live with them anymore but when Paulie came home the apartment came alive. Even Papa smiled. Papa never said much; he had his job for the government, his books and cared not a jot what he wore. Amélie was like Papa and Paulie was a mini-Maman when it came to being noticed in a crowd. That's what Maman's friends said and Maman had lots and lots of friends.

Amélie's mother was a never-ending bubbling swirl of laughter and disaster, the arrondissement's best dresser and worst cooker. It made Amélie happy just to be with her, even when she served up her burnt, blackened dinners or scolded Amélie for being dull, the worst crime in Madame Dreyfus's world. At least it was until the Nazis arrived.

Life was not so simple anymore. Papa lost his job. His bosses, Frenchmen like him, said there was no room for 'people of his type' in the government. Amélie had never thought of her family as a 'type' and now they were. All of a sudden she was different to her best friend Madeleine and Madeleine began looking at her funny.

For this weekend they could forget all that. Paulie was home for Papa's birthday, which meant games of hide-and-seek and her hiding place that no-one ever discovered. The trick was to come out of it unseen and then duck behind a curtain or under the bed to emerge in triumph from there when the others gave up. And never, ever reveal your secret.

Amélie was good at keeping secrets. She sucked in the smell of her mother once more. Her legs were beginning to ache from crouching on the little shelf at the back of the giant wardrobe; the largest piece of furniture in the block the concierge informed Amélie the day they watched six sweating men heave it up the stairs. Amélie believed it had to be big because everything about Maman was large. Being hugged by Maman, clutched tight into her, it felt like all your worries were squeezed away.

Amélie took after her father, long legged and gangly, neither quite comfortable in their own bodies as if they'd forgotten to try them on before choosing. My baby giraffe, Maman called Amélie.

By now, Amélie was sure, Maman would have given up seeking and collapsed into an armchair with an exhausted sigh, calling on Papa to fix her a pre-lunch drink and complaining about the heat. In summers gone, before the Nazis came, they would have left Paris and its baking city heat and gone to the beach where Maman's British half would float to the surface and she'd roll up her dress and tuck it into her bloomers to paddle with Amélie. Maman had lived most of her life in France and become more French, or rather Parisian, than the French. Except on holiday where having a British father meant always being a Britisher at the seaside. Sometimes Amélie's Grandfather – always Grandfather, never Grandpere – would come too and make great big sandcastles with his daughter and granddaughter.

If only they could live in a castle now, thought Amélie, as she let go of the fur coat. Shut themselves away until the Nazis were gone, pull up the drawbridge and get ready to pour boiling hot oil on any Boche who tried to get in. She giggled – the word Boche was banned by the Germans. They didn't like to be called names. So her mother called them the Hun, as the British had in the Great War.

"Amélieeeeeeee."

Her brother's sing-song voice breezed through the apartment. He performed in night clubs but told her she was too young to go and see him.

"Amélieeeee, where are you… we can't find you… I'm…"

What he was going to say, or do, Amélie never found out

4

because he was interrupted by a thunderous knock on the front door.

Heavy footsteps trod into the apartment. "What on earth…" Amélie heard her mother begin before being cut off by a barked command. There was no more talking only the sound of heavy boots around the apartment. Heavy boots coming into her parent's bedroom, coming to the wardrobe, stopping. She waited for the click of the latch.

It didn't come. Instead the boots retreated, the front door slammed. Silence.

Chapter 2

Amélie didn't know how long she hid, crouched on the tiny shelf at the back of her mother's colossal wardrobe. Her legs yelled a silent protest at the torture she was putting them through. She didn't notice because she was frozen. The wardrobe door may have remained tight shut but fear had found a way in and seized hold of her.

At last fear let go, just a little but enough. She unlatched the cupboard door – that was its secret, you could open it from the inside – and the door swung open.

It was late afternoon. She could tell by the sun on the bedroom wall. She stepped out of the wardrobe, sat on the bed and rubbed feeling back into her legs. She stood up, testing her legs like a baby giraffe. They worked, just the same as before. She wondered around the apartment.

Nothing had changed. Everything was as before. Except she was alone.

The sun streamed through the apartment windows. Being on the top floor, their home soaked up the heat of the afternoon sunshine. Usually, Maman would have lent out the windows and pulled the shutters almost closed. Dust danced in the sunbeams, the noise of normal life rose from the street below: the stutter of a car engine, the shout of a children's game, the distant bark of a dog, the clang of a church bell.

Inside the apartment there was not a sound. A cup of coffee sat on the kitchen table. Amélie put out a hand and touched it. Cold. She was thirsty, her throat parched. She turned on the tap. It pounded into the sink like a waterfall. She turned it off as quick as she could. Something was telling her she had to be quiet, quiet as a mouse. She felt like she'd done something bad, her stomach churned.

Amélie sat down at the kitchen table and looked along the hall. She noticed the front door had not been properly closed. The Germans must have slammed it so hard it bounced open again. She crossed the hall and peaked out, a door snapped shut somewhere below. She pushed the front door to, not daring to close it in case it made a noise. She sat down in the kitchen again, licked her lips, took a glass from the cabinet and let a trickle of water fill it. She gulped it down before crossing to the kitchen window. It opened onto a small balcony where Maman grew herbs in pots. She didn't dare step outside. Instead she peered down through the window to the street.

Outside nothing seemed out of the ordinary. Inside everything seemed ordinary. Apart from the silence; home was never silent. Amélie shivered. There was menace in the stillness. She tried to whistle a soft tune, something to fight the silence, but her mouth and lips were already dry again.

She went back to her parents' room, took the fur coat from its hanger and laid it on the floor of the wardrobe. She closed the door and wrapped herself in it, closed her eyes, pressed them tight together, the fur of the coat tickling her chin. This shouldn't be happening. She kept her eyes squeezed shut.

The back of the wardrobe swung open and Amélie stepped through. "There you are," said Maman. Her family, Maman, Papa and Paul, were sitting around the breakfast table in the villa they rented for summers by the sea. If she stood still and held her breath she could hear the whisper of waves, just over the sand dune visible through the open windows.

Her brother paused dunking a large piece of croissant into his hot chocolate to wish her "Bonjour!" Paulie always sounded like he was about to burst into song when he said good day. Papa looked up from his newspaper and nodded an unspoken bonjour. He didn't like to talk until he'd finished the business pages. Maman was wearing one of her summer dresses, Cordoba-coloured with white polka dots, all the rage that summer. She beamed and patted the empty chair next to her.

Amélie sat down but sat only on thin air as the chair disappeared, followed by Maman and Paulie and then the table. Her father looked up, doffed his hat, muttered "Au revoir" and with that he too faded into nothing.

She woke with a start, eyes blinking at the darkness of the cupboard. If she blinked hard enough she might bring back the light, might bring back Maman and Paulie and Papa.

Amélie sat up. "Papa never wore a hat indoors," she said and opened the wardrobe door.

It was morning, early. She stared at the coffee cup on the kitchen table, its surface sprinkled with dust.

"Non," she said. She made a decision. "I will not hide."

She emptied the cup down the sink, returned to the wardrobe, hung up the fur coat and closed the door. She glanced out the window. The hot spell had broken; looked like rain. She sounded like Papa. She pulled on her coat.

The Yellow Star stared at the room. It stood out on her left breast, its six points marking her. Pointing out she was not the same as *them*.

She looked down at herself. Why was she different? They'd never been different before. What Father believed in, well, it had never seemed to matter and it wasn't often she even noticed it. She liked it when he got the candlesticks out for Hanukkah and gave her a handful of coins with his serious face. Maman would make potato pancakes and they'd smother them in apricot jam. Sometimes he complained to Maman about her not cooking how she was supposed to cook and for the next few days she would serve the food as he wanted.

Amélie picked at a thread holding one end of the Star's uppermost point. It loosened quickly and she heard her mother's 'tsk'. She despaired trying to get Amélie neat and tidy to go out on to the streets of Paris.

"People here, they judge you as soon as they look at you," Maman would say in her primest voice. "Non, non, non, there can be no loose ends. I detest loose ends."

Amélie patted down the thread, feeling the roughness of the material on the smoothness of her summer coat. "Eh bien," she said aloud, trying to find a jolly note as Maman always did. "Allez."

She eased the front door carefully open, wedged it shut behind her with a folded piece of paper – the keys had disappeared – and tiptoed down the stairs. The concierge's room, from where the old woman kept an eye on the block's comings and goings, was empty. Amélie scurried past and out on to the street.

A German poster was plastered on the wall across the street listing the many things citizens of occupied Paris were not allowed to do on pain of death. Amélie ignored it, turned right and made her way to their local café. She wasn't sure if everyone was staring at her – or rather at her Star – but that's what it felt like.

She summoned a cheery "Bonjour" for Marcel behind the counter and ordered a croissant and a glass of milk. He brought her breakfast to her table in the window.

"Combien?" wondered Amélie, holding out a handful of coins she'd found on the table by the apartment's front door. Marcel shook his head then bent forward and whispered in her ear.

"I saw them taken – it's not safe for you to come here, not any more, you must go, please… when you have eaten. Please… I don't want any trouble."

He retreated behind the counter without looking at her. Amélie chewed on her croissant, it felt dry, gulped down her milk and wiped a sleeve across her face to get rid of any milk moustache. Maman would have scolded her for that. Maman loved to sit outside a café, dressed up to the nines, and share a sticky pastry with Amélie – always the same instruction to the waiter, 'two forks, M'sieur, if you please' – and watch Paris go by. But not for long because Maman was part of Paris and she wanted others to watch her go by. Amélie returned her cup and plate to the counter and left the café without a word.

For the first time there were tears in her eyes as she walked back towards the apartment. She tried to blink them away. She felt sick, she wanted Maman to come home and put her to bed, pop a clove of garlic under her tongue like she did when there was flu about. A woman, a concerned frown on her face, walked towards her, saw the Yellow Star and swerved away.

The concierge was back on watch. Amélie walked past the entrance to her block. She didn't want the concierge seeing her. She didn't want anyone to know where she was because the Germans would be hunting for her. She was on her own now; Amélie Dreyfus against Germany.

Chapter 3

Amélie walked and walked, left behind her arrondissement, with its great white cathedral rising above Paris, and trod down the hill towards the centre of the city. She tried to concentrate, think about where she was going even though she didn't really know, didn't have a plan. She needed one. If she appeared lost someone might try and help her and when they saw the Star…

She covered it with her hand as a man bustled past her. He didn't notice her. That was one small thing in her favour – and there were precious few of those – most adults don't see children, not really. Come a time like this and they see even less, becoming so wrapped in themselves they don't look around. They're too afraid of what they might see.

That was one of the lessons Amélie had learnt about

being on the streets. There, that was another thing in her favour and one Maman and Papa would have been horrified to find out: Amélie had stopped going to school more than a month earlier.

"Paris is a German town now," blared another large poster. The city looked the same but it had changed. At school, at home...

Every household was ordered to fill in a form and declare if they were Jewish or not. Amélie had listened to her parents arguing. "We do not break the law," insisted her father. "We are French and France protects *all* her people."

These are not our laws, roared her mother in response. "And your France... your France is gone – do you not understand, husband?"

Papa's voice remained as it always did. "It is who we are and I will not hide that from anyone..." He paused and Amélie saw him shake his head. "C'est moi. It is me – I am not ashamed, and I am not scared by them." He filled in the form and their lives began to change.

She passed a park where Paulie used to take her at weekends. "INTERDIT AUX JUIFS" announced a sign. No Jews. They weren't allowed to go to the cinema or the music hall. On the Metro they could only travel in the last carriage and, most infuriating to Maman, they were only allowed to shop for one hour in the afternoon, once everyone else had their pick.

"But how will they know I am a Jew – I look no different to Madeleine," said Amélie.

The Germans had thought of that. They made them wear the Yellow Star.

School changed after that. She was teased for being different, even Madeleine stopped wanting to be with her: 'I can't Amélie, it is dangerous for me to be your friend.'

There was one teacher, Monseiur Leclerc, who decided he would not teach Jews. Amélie and three boys were made to stand and face the wall with hands on their heads. It felt to Amélie like they were surrendering and she wasn't going to surrender to anyone. So she stopped going to school and took to the streets instead.

One day a boy, about her brother's age, thrust a leaflet in her hand and told her to give it to her papa. She read it. 'Hide your children,' it said, 'because the Nazis are coming for the Jews'. She ran home and showed it to her father. He crumpled it up and threw it in the bin. 'Nonsense,' he said. Amélie saw fear in his eyes. He didn't know what was going on any more than she did.

Amélie's legs were hurting with all the walking. She passed a queue outside a butcher's shop. The women stared hawk-like at her, suspecting she was looking for a chance to push in ahead of them. The sun came out and the temperature rose; summer in Paris can be scorching. Amélie unbuttoned her coat and was about to take it off when she remembered she wasn't allowed to. She didn't have a Star on her blouse and she had to show a Star at all times. That was the law.

It was with relief she hurried into the narrow streets of the Marais. The sun struggled to reach down here. It felt like this part of the city was hunkered down and in hiding. She turned into the Rue Charlot, passing number six where she liked to pause with Paulie to watch the old clockmaker at work and listen to the constant ding and dong as clock after clock chimed different hours.

It seemed to Amélie that each clock believed it was right and the others wrong but were nevertheless happy to share a shelf with those telling a different time. Much like all the different people who lived in Paris, they were right and the neighbours wrong but they all got along in the end. Got along until the Germans came. Today the shop was shuttered and made not a sound.

She turned into Rouelle Sourdis as if this was where she always intended to come and stopped outside the club where her brother sang. It too appeared closed. A door opened and a young man emerged. He clutched an umbrella and was dressed much like her brother but sported a smear of a moustache.

"'Allo, Freddie?" she said, her voice wobbling with uncertainty. "Have you seen Paulie?"

Freddie looked at her and she could see his eye drawn to the Star.

"Please," she said.

He shook his head, one quick shake as if he didn't want to be seen communicating with her.

"Aidez moi," she added.

He shrugged and hurried away without a word. At the end of the street, he turned out of sight without looking back.

"Help me," she said again, this time her voice no more than a whisper. Her head was light. She stumbled back down the street and found a small café. She slumped into a seat at one of the two outdoor tables. A waiter came out and she showed him her handful of coins. He shook his head and retreated indoors. She could hear a woman's voice, cross, scolding the waiter. A minute later and the owner of the voice emerged. She smiled at Amélie and put a plate in front of her, on it a tear of baguette, some cheese and a pear.

"Eat, my dear," she said and placed a comforting hand on Amélie's shoulder.

She tried to eat slowly, savour each mouthful, mix a slither of pear with a crumble of cheese, but she wanted to get home, to hurry home and lock the door behind her. She wanted to get back in the wardrobe where no-one could find her.

They found her on the way home. Ahead she saw a checkpoint, a small queue and German soldiers checking papers, turned hurriedly on to the Rue de Moussy and walked into a trap.

Two more soldiers, in grey uniforms, helmets low on their eyes, were waiting in a doorway for anyone trying to avoid the checkpoint. A heavy hand fell on Amélie's shoulder, the same shoulder the waitress had touched tenderly minutes before. She winced as the soldier dug his fingers in. Her hand leapt instinctively to cover her Star.

"Where you darting off to then…" The soldier let go of her shoulder and instead pulled her hand away, gripping her wrist tightly… "Juden."

Chapter 4

Amélie glanced up in turn at her captors. She was walking between them, their leather boots creaking with each step. Their necks were red, rubbed raw by the stiff collars on their heavy uniforms and their faces were red too. One had a bead of sweat dribbling from beneath his helmet. The other, she noticed, had dark lines beneath the fingernails of the hand that clutched her shoulder, in case she should be tempted to try and dart away. Maman detested dirty fingernails.

Amélie felt tiny, insignificant between them. But if she was insignificant why were they bothering about her?

They marched down the Rue de Rivoli, the buildings growing and sprucing themselves up as they progressed towards a smarter arrondissement. People looked away as they passed, nobody wanted to get involved with the fate of a Jewish girl. It wasn't worth it, they had to protect themselves.

The little and large trio crossed the Place de la Concorde and entered one of the grand buildings on its far side from where the Germans ruled France and its capital. Amélie's feet ached, her mind a daze, as though it'd switched off because there was no point now she was in the hands of the Boche.

No one seemed to know what to do with her. After a while she was taken upstairs, to a small room on the top floor with a window looking over the rooftops. A large dog was ushered in with her and commanded to sit opposite her. It remained standing.

"Wait here," barked the guard. "If you move the Alsatian will attack you." He began to close the door.

"It's a Malinois." Amélie spoke without thinking. She loved dogs, had wanted one for as long as she could remember, read every book she could find in the library and for a while taken an imaginary one for walks – much to Paulie's amusement.

"What?" said the guard, pausing with the door half closed.

"Malinois, not an Alsatian."

The guard, a young man with a pointed face, frowned. He wasn't going to be outsmarted by a child, especially one with a star on her coat. "How should I know, came with the building – but what I do know is that if you move a muscle it will tear you to bits, starting with your face." He grinned horribly and slammed the door. Amélie listened to the key turning the lock.

The dog wondered over to the door and sniffed at the keyhole. 'Malinois are from Belgium, they are first and foremost sheepdogs and were used by the French and Belgian armies in the Great War to find wounded soldiers…' in her head Amélie recited what she remembered from her book of breeds. Better that than think about where she was and what was going to happen to her. She wasn't even really listening to her own thoughts. 'They are very intelligent and respond well to firm commands.'

Amélie looked at the dog. Definitely a Malinois. She thought it not long fully grown. He had a black muzzle and pointed alert ears, the rest of him was light brown. The dog looked at Amélie, head cocked to one side. 'Respond well to firm commands.'

"Asseyez-vous," said Amélie.

The dog remained standing.

"Asseyez-vous!" Amélie tried again, her voice this time as stern as she could manage.

At once the dog sat.

Amélie smiled.

"Good boy," she said.

Amélie slid off her chair and knelt on the floor. The dog growled but stayed still. She held out a hand, an offering to the dog.

"So you belong to nobody now, ma chérie…"

The dog leaned forward and sniffed at her hand. Slowly she leaned forward too and rubbed behind his ear. The dog angled his head so she could get to the exact spot he wanted tickled.

After a few moments, the dog lay down and rolled on to its back, nodding down at its tummy as if saying 'there please, tickle me there.' As she stroked the soft fur of the Malinois' stomach, Amélie studied the window. It didn't appear to have a lock on it; after all they were on the sixth floor.

She gave the dog a last rub, patted his stomach and stood up.

'What you doing?' said the dog's eyes as they followed her across the room.

She opened the window and looked out. They were at the back of the building. The roof dropped away but not far. The smoothly tiled surface angled down to a wide gutter and then rose again to make a V-shape before being interrupted by another small window opposite Amélie. She grinned.

"So long dog," she said and gave him a last rub behind the ear. He wagged his tail and watched her pull herself up and out the window then whined at her departure. Amélie clung on to the window ledge and lowered herself down towards the gutter. She would have to let go and slide the last part, hoping the gutter would hold her weight.

That was not all she had to hope; she had to hope the window on the opposite side of the roof was unlocked, the room it opened onto empty, unlocked, and that she could find a way from that room to the street... A long list and one best not thought about. What choice did she have? Sit in the room with the dog until they came to take her away?

And then what would happen to her? There were rumours, dark whispers, about camps in the east. The boy who'd handed out the leaflets had told her they were true. Others scoffed at the suggestion, dismissed it as scaremongering. Well, she was not going to sit around waiting to find out who was right.

She let go of the ledge and her hands pressed against the tiles to try and slow her descent.

"Owww." Her left ankle twisted as it reached the gutter. The gutter creaked but held. Amélie lent back against the roof and rubbed her ankle, contemplating the next part of her escape plan. The roof was easy to slide down, not so easy to climb up.

The dog's head appeared at the window. "Good boy," said Amélie as loud as she dared. If the dog started barking she was done for. The sound of traffic out the front of the building drifted up to her. Above the clouds had cleared – as if keen to get away from the occupied city – and a china blue sky looked down on her.

Amélie looked up at the window on the other side. She stretched. It was out of reach. There was nothing to grip on to help her clamber up to the window. She tried to scramble up and slid back down. She made another unsuccessful attempt.

She wiped a hand across her brow. She was sweating and her mouth was dry. She couldn't reach the window. There was a whine above her. She looked up to see the dog halfway out the window. He seemed stuck.

"Non," said Amélie, wagging a finger at him. "Non, non."

The dog wasn't stuck. With one more scramble of his back legs he tipped himself out of the window and slid down the roof until he hit Amélie. Together in a tumble of legs and arms, with legs outnumbering arms three to one, they slithered into the gutter.

Amélie felt the wetness of the gutter soak one arm, while the dog tried to soak her face with his eager licking.

"Off," she said, trying to push him away. "Get off me, Felix."

She pushed herself up into an awkward crouch and wrapped her arms around the dog's neck. He seemed like a Felix to her. Maman had taken her to the circus once, bustling through the crowd down Faubourg Saint Antoine and into the big top. Felix had been the strongman, lifting massive dumbbells that drooped with the weights piled on each end while the crowd 'ooood' and 'aaahhhhed.'

The Malinois reminded her of Felix, big and strong. The dog's tail beat a rhythm against the tiles. He was happy to be reunited with his new friend.

"Big and strong," thought Amélie and looked up at the window, so close but not close enough.

"Big and strong."

The idea surged through her mind, skipping the planning stages, the doubt department, the don't-be-so-ridiculous room. She had no choice; get out or be caught like a soon-to-be-dead rat in a trap.

25

"Here," she said to Felix and made him stand. She rubbed behind his ear and stroked down his back then stood up. This had to be done quickly, before the dog realised what was happening.

"Stay," she said and pointed a commanding finger at Felix.

Amélie was fleet of foot. Where she'd got that from she'd no idea, certainly not Maman and she'd never seen any sign of it from Papa either. But she was and it allowed her to place one foot on the dog's back, issue another stern "Stay" and before Felix could protest, leap upwards using the dog's back as a jumping-off platform.

Her hands stretched before her and her fingers felt for and grasped the window ledge. She hung on. Felix thought it was a game and tugged at her shoe, letting out a playful growl.

"Non," she said, "Down, get down."

She kicked out with her other foot and caught poor Felix on the chin. The dog yelped and let go of her other foot. Amélie pushed at the window and there wasn't even time to feel relief as it flew open and she flew through it, landing in a heap on the floor in puff of dust. The room was empty and seemed to have been so for some time.

"Rrrrrruuuffff."

Felix wanted her back. He barked again, this time louder. Amélie glanced out the window to 'sush' him and found herself looking straight at someone else who wanted her back.

"Halt," yelled the guard from the other window and pointed a pistol at her. Amélie ducked. The guard shouted something else, which even if it had been in French rather than angry German Amélie wouldn't have hung around to listen to.

She darted for the door. It opened on her first try. She was through it seconds before a bullet cracked into the wall of the corridor. There was a staircase at one end. Amélie ran for it.

The staircase was circular. She glanced down, trying to slow her breathing so she could listen. She could still make out the shouts of the guard and Felix's barking back on the roof. But inside her building… nothing.

She tore down the stairs, taking them two at a time. Her footsteps sounded thunderous but they were the only footsteps she could hear.

At the bottom the steps curved down and ended at a door. She tried the handle. The door wouldn't budge. She pulled as hard as she could, desperate. There were boots on the staircase.

"HALT!" A loud voice echoed down the stairwell as she rattled the door.

"Open, open, open… please," said Amélie feeling tears building up behind her eyes. So close, so close.

She glanced up, trying to keep the tears in. There – a bolt. She stretched up, on her tiptoes. It was in reach. She slid it back and pulled again. Still the door wouldn't budge. The footsteps were getting louder, the click-clunk of heavy boots with iron-rimmed soles.

Another bolt on the bottom. With a sob she slid it back and this time the door opened. She raced out into an alley, didn't even look both ways, just chose one and scarpered, emerging on to a busy road. Beyond it and over a waist-high wall, she knew, was the river, the Seine.

Amélie ran. A car shrieked to a halt, a man's angry voice accompanying her across the road. She reached the wall, placed one hand on top and without looking leapt.

Chapter 5

She expected the soft landing of the water. The Seine was deep and swift but she was a good swimmer. That's what came of long summers by the sea.

She was wrong. She'd forgotten the path that led along the banks of the river.

The landing drove what little breath she had left from her body and twisted her ankle. Pain shot up her leg but the will to survive was all the medicine she needed. Amélie was not going to let them take her. She had to get away. Because she had to be home when Maman and Papa and Paulie came back.

Tears were running freely down her face, covered in red dust from the path; her clothes were dirty and crumpled from her escape, a streak of gutter mud down her raincoat. Her nose was snotty. She wiped the back of her hand across her face. What would Maman think if she could see her?

Amélie smiled through the tears and forced herself up. She hobbled down the path, each step drawing a gasp of pain. A small arch appeared, about the height of a man's waist, dug under the road, dank and dirty. She disappeared into its darkness and crouched down against the far wall, pressing into the corner, trying to ignore the smell, trying to make herself as small as possible; Amélie the Invisible.

She listened, attempting to slow her breathing. Dogs, men's voices, stern and angry, approaching the arch. The voices grew louder and she saw the silhouette of a dog at the entrance and a pair of legs, the snarl of a command and the dog was let off the leash. It raised its muzzle and sniffed then trotted into the arch, tail wagging.

The dog came straight for Amélie, tail still wagging. Felix. She reached out and stroked his head, ran her fingers behind his ear and tickled. She gave him a final pat.

"Go," she said and waved a hand at him. Felix sat down, as if deciding what he should do.

"*Wer ist da?*" The words were barked at Felix. Two pairs of boots stood at the arch.

"Go," repeated Amélie, this time a little louder. She leaned forward and gave him a gentle push. Felix nodded, at least that's what it looked like to Amélie, and when his handler shouted a command he trotted out.

The dog disappeared and the legs followed. Amélie stayed where she was. Stillness returned to the riverbank. Above the arch she could hear the rumble of traffic on the road. Then the hoot of a barge's horn followed by the lulling chugga-chugga of its engine as it pottered past.

Amélie shuffled over to the entrance and glanced out.

"Oh la la!" said a woman, surprised by the sudden appearance of this wild-eyed, dirty-looking child.

Amélie raised a finger to her lips and limped as fast as she could down the path, taking the opposite direction to the Germans and their dogs.

When she was sure she was safe – for the time being at least – she stopped under the arc of a bridge. She sat on a bench and removed her coat. It did not take long to do what she wanted. Her mother was not good at sewing and the thread was easily picked away.

Amélie put her coat back on and walked to the water's edge. She held the Star in her right hand. She looked down at it then tried to crumple it in her palm but as soon as she opened her hand, the six points curled back into position.

She threw it as hard as she could, grunting as she did so. The Star did not go far but it made the water, landing with barely a ripple. She'd expected it to sink. She assumed because it weighed her down it would sink all the way to the bottom. Instead it floated away on the grey water. Perhaps it was an omen, a good one and she needed a good omen. She didn't want to sink.

The Yellow Star disappeared from view and seemed to take the last of her strength with her. Her head spun, she lent forward over the water and for a moment thought she was going to follow the Star, and for a moment she didn't mind if she did.

Amélie shook her head and stepped back. She staggered to the bench and sat down, leaning forward, cradling her head in her hands. After a while the dizziness passed, replaced by an overwhelming desire to sleep. She lifted her legs on to the bench, laid her hands together as a pillow and closed her eyes.

Another dream; on the beach and in the distance her family, carrying rugs and picnic baskets.

"Wait," called out Amélie. "Maman, Paulie… stop, I'm coming."

Maman turned around. Amélie could see she was trying to shout something but her words were carried away on the sea breeze. Paulie waved at her and gestured for her to hurry.

"Wait for me," yelled Amélie.

She hurried after them, then hurried some more, then ran, then ran as fast as she could, as fast as she'd ever run. But Maman and Papa and Paulie came no closer and for some reason they would not stop and wait. They were walking quicker than she could run and soon they dropped below the horizon.

"Wait," shouted Amélie one last time but she knew they wouldn't.

Chapter 6

Where was she? Champs-Élysées, the faded yellow teddy bear she'd had since she was a baby, was in her arms. She hugged him tight while her sleepy mind stirred into action.

She was in the apartment, home, in her own bed, wearing her own nightie. Those dreams, those terrible dreams, had filled her mind. She lay there and tried to put everything in order. Her arrest and escape; maybe that was a dream. She ran a hand down her leg and felt her ankle. Ouch.

Her painful stagger home came back to her, unseen through the dark, through the curfew – no-one was allowed out after dark. If luck was rationed like bread and sugar she'd used up all hers yesterday. But she'd survived hadn't she? For a handful of days. Who knows how long it would be before the war ended and Maman, Papa and Paulie could come home.

She opened her bedroom cupboard and tugged down her suitcase. In it she put Champs-Élysées, with one last kiss on his furry head, her diary, her favourite necklace and ring – a gift from Maman last birthday – and a few other pits and pieces. On top of it all she folded in Maman's fur coat before clicking the case shut.

She carried it through to the bathroom, found the loose floorboard, lifted it up and slid the suitcase into the space below. It would stay there, she decided, until this war was ended.

In the kitchen she opened all the cupboards and began a stock-take, placing anything edible on the table. She'd enough for a couple of weeks, maybe three if she cut out lunch, and none of it would be fresh. She found the family ration cards but they were no good to her – there was a large, red J stamped on each. Hand those over and she'd be back in German hands in no time.

To stay alive she had to be careful: hours of boredom punctuated by terror and a feeling of isolation. At first she went out little, staring at the door in expectant horror every time she heard the heavy tread of boots on the stairs. She never wore shoes indoors because she didn't want any sounds of life to reach the apartment below. Just in case.

The doorbell rang once. Amélie kept quiet and after two more rings the visitor gave up. She pressed her ear against the door to make sure whoever it was had gone. All she heard was her own breathing.

Finally, as her food began to run out – she was down to one meal a day of rice or lentils with a spoonful of something from the dwindling supply of tinned food – she had to go out. She found the front door key and taking a necklace of her mother's slid the silver Star of David off the chain and in its place threaded the key. She hung it round her neck and added the star along with the rest of her mother's jewellery to the suitcase under the floorboards.

Outside she felt freer without the Star on her coat. But at the same time more frightened. On the bad days it made her feel sick. She was breaking the rules and that felt wrong – she got that from Papa she thought, he would never break a single rule.

Yet without the Star she could be invisible on the streets, might be able to survive on the streets; but what if someone spotted her, someone who knew her, what if the soldiers or the police could tell, what if they could tell she was Jewish? Could they tell she was Jewish? When she shivered she wasn't sure if it was because she was cold or because she was scared.

One damp morning, with her chin hunched down into the neck of her coat, she watched a column of prisoners, French soldiers in torn and shabby uniforms, being marched towards the station. A soldier with a crutch under one arm slipped and fell. His fellow soldiers marched on, stepping past him as he scrabbled for his crutch.

Amélie stepped forward from the small, silent crowd gathered on the pavement. She put an arm around the man's skinny shoulders and tried to help him up.

"NEIN!" A guard approached at the run, yelling at her in German. Amélie turned away from him and continued trying to help the man back to his feet.

"My crutch… my crutch…" he groaned.

Amélie nearly had the man up when the guard reached them. She'd her back to him so didn't see what he did. But she felt it. His boot sent her flying. She hit the cobbled street hard, pain shot along her arms and screamed from her knees.

"NEIN!" he yelled again and towered over her. He raised his rifle. Amélie turned her head and looked up at his snarling face and she knew then, in that moment as her pain was pushed aside by a rage in her belly, that survival, living only to survive, was not enough.

She would not accept being scared all the time. She would fight back, fight them with every last breath she had in her body, for what the soldier had done to her, for what they'd done to this poor prisoner and most of all for taking Maman and Papa and Paulie away. Somehow she would fight them. She'd find a way.

Hands grabbed her and pulled her upright, two women from the crowd. Behind the guard two prisoners were scooping up the wounded man and his crutch. The guard kept his rifle pointed at Amélie. The women clutched Amélie between them. The three of them faced the guard.

"Walk back with us… slowly," whispered one of the women. Amélie's head was spinning. She would fight them. Her knees were throbbing, blood ran down her legs. "Shhhh," added the woman as if sensing Amélie was about to scream her defiance.

The other woman put her free hand out towards the soldier and gestured palm down 'keep calm, everybody just keep calm…' She tried a tight smile. The soldier kept his rifle aimed at Amélie. They were back on the pavement. The crowd parted, no-one else wanted to be part of this.

A command was barked from the far side of the road and the soldier spun round. An officer gestured at him to march on – the column was nearly past. The soldier muttered something and shouldered his rifle. As he marched past he turned to glare at Amélie, who grinned at him and stuck her tongue out.

"Non," hissed one of the woman and tugged her away, behind the crowd and down an alleyway. But not before Amélie saw the angry redness return to the soldier's face and that made her feel just a little bit better.

"You are crazy," said the woman as she sat Amélie down on a doorstep. "Or stupid. Last week a girl, young like you, was sent to prison for doing that."

"Non," said Amélie.

"Oui," insisted the woman. "I read it. They lock you up."

She took out a handkerchief and dabbed at Amélie's bleeding knees.

"Pah, that is no good – I'll take you home, your Maman can patch you up. Where do you…"

Amélie stood up, ignoring the pain in her knees. "Non," she said. "Thank you for everything, you are very kind but I must go."

She pushed away the woman's hand and ran down the alley. She didn't need mothers fussing over her, treating her as a child. Not when Amélie Dreyfus was going to war.

But how? That was the question that troubled and trapped her once she'd got home, dabbed her wounds clean

– hissing at the stinging – and calmed down. Over the next few days she racked her brains, poured over Papa's history books. How? The best idea she could come up with was putting sugar in the petrol tanks of German trucks and cars. But she'd run out of sugar.

She took to the streets. If she couldn't fight yet she could prepare for the fight and that meant learning every corner of the battleground – she read that in one of Papa's books about Napoleon. She would get to know as much of Paris as much she could, find every hiding place, every short cut.

She sang to herself as she walked, softly, a quiet note of defiance. It was a song popular in the last summer before war came, when everyone thought Hitler a jumped-up little nincompoop with a silly moustache. When its tune crackled out of the radio, everybody joined in, whistling where they didn't know the words.

"House painters are mostly good guys.
There is one, though, who is quite mad."

She walked and walked through a gloomy city, from her home at the top of Montmartre down into Pigalle, where the only smiles came from off-duty soldiers playing at tourists. Parisians grimaced and hurried on, staring at their shoes.

"He's a big bad wolf.
Oh ho oh ho, he's two bricks short of a bad."

On to the river she went, with its ponderous barges steaming by, past the brooding bulk of the great cathedral of Notre Dame and over to the south bank, the Latin Quartier and Montparnasse, turning down alleyways and climbing narrow steps, exploring the railway bridges and arches that led to Paris's six great stations.

"According to my sister he has delusions of grandeur.

Oh ho oh ho, he's a jumped up Attila."

Train stations, their windows painted war-time blue, Amélie discovered were always busy so there was always a crowd and a crowd is a good place to hide. Except the Germans knew that so stations were crawling with soldiers and the leather coats of the Gestapo, the feared secret police hunting for Jews and anyone else who shouldn't be there.

"He's sick with something, much worse than gas, oh ho oh ho.

It seems to pain him. He calls it 'living space'... oh ho oh ho."

They never thought he would come. Not after the last time, the Great War, the War to End All Wars. Nobody wanted that again. That's what everyone said. But it turns out Hitler wasn't listening to them. And here he was.

"Oh ho oh ho, one who is quite maaaaddd..."

* * *

The sun seemed to have been banished from Paris for the rest of that summer, in its place grey skies hung over the capital, German grey, like the uniforms the soldiers wore. Amélie was still scared, but she learnt to live with it, day by day, and she learnt to be cautious – she could not afford another mistake. If she blundered into another checkpoint she would be finished.

Maman's stock of food was gone. Some days Amélie begged but she had to be sharp eyed for Gendarmes, the police who liked nothing better than to deliver a hard clip round the ears. She grew thinner and day-dreamed of food, big steaming plates of, well, anything as long as there was lots of it. Most of all she wanted a Sunday treat, a crepe rolled up and filled with creamy chocolate that spilled down her fork and made her fingers sticky.

"Tsk, tsk," Maman would say as Amélie licked them clean.

"Tsk, tsk," muttered Amélie as she watched a girl, about her age, pocket a couple of apples from a market stall when the woman's back was turned. Her tummy rumbled a round of applause. Amélie approached the stall. The woman turned around and glared at her. She walked away heart thumping, tummy grumbling.

Chapter 7

Somehow she survived. On not very much. Some days she struck lucky. She would stand outside a café looking sad, lost and lonely – not a difficult act – and every now and then a waitress would wave her to the back door and hand her a plate of this and that, a couple of mouthfuls of bread, a mouse-sized piece of cheese or, if her luck was really in, yesterday's croissant and a smudge of jam. Once she was even given a bowl of soup.

For a time, almost a happy time, she teamed up with another street girl, Nina. They haunted the back streets behind the smart restaurants off the Champs-Élysées where the German officers ate, the two of them searching the bins for leftovers and plate scrapings. On some nights the smell drifting from the kitchens made their heads spin.

It was Nina's idea to sing. They would make a sign –

43

something made-up, like the 'Fabulous Singing Sisters from the Circus du Monde' – put it next to a hat then stand on the steps leading to the Sacré-Cœur or in the gardens around the Tour Eiffel and sing.

"We hide in plain sight, see?" said Nina. Amélie knew Nina was on the run too but didn't know why. They didn't speak about things like that. Amélie was learning you had to be careful with knowledge.

Nina chose the songs. If there were officers around they would sing sweet songs and the officers would think of their sweet children back home in Germany and drop a handful of coins in the hat. For the younger men they sung jolly tunes and Nina even taught Amélie a well-known German folk song. The young Boche loved that and the coins would clink into the hat. One afternoon they made enough to share a dinner in a café back in the maze of the Marais. The proprietor insisted they pay first before he brought out a chewy piece of chicken and some squidgy carrots. It tasted like a feast fit for a Queen fallen on hard times.

Then one morning Nina wasn't there anymore. She didn't turn up at their usual meeting place, halfway down the steps off the Rue Lepic. Amélie returned the next day, and for the rest of the week. No Nina. On the last morning a man in a leather coat was waiting in their usual spot. Amélie walked on by and never came back.

That was the end of the singing. Amélie didn't have the courage to do it on her own, and anyway it was Nina who had the true singing voice. "Voice of an angel," Maman would have said.

Some nights Amélie would cry, sob into her pillow, wishing Maman would open the bedroom door and cuddle her until she was over her "night frights", humming a song until she drifted away. When she woke she would lie in bed for a while and harden herself for the day ahead. There were better days, but the nights were always long.

One morning she pulled back the floorboards in the bathroom and took out Champs-Élysées. Nights weren't quite so bad after that.

Summer was beginning to say so-long, as usual in Paris a long-drawn out adieu. Some days were still warm; on others there was a chill in the air. And when you are hungry the world feels colder. Most of Paris was hungry.

Amélie began spending her days in museums, which meant less time for begging and scavenging but she felt too tired and too chilly to spend long on the streets. She liked the hush of the museums, an oasis of calm from the storms raging outside their thick walls. She was too weary to try and fight the Germans just at the moment – though that flame still flickered inside her. She wouldn't let it go out.

She tried to be careful and divide her time between museums. She didn't want to be noticed but in the Musée de l'Homme she was.

Amélie saw a young woman staring at her, eyes accompanying her around the room. There was one other person there; an elderly man sat on a bench studying a full-length skeleton from hundreds, probably thousands of years ago.

Amélie edged towards the door, pretending she was eyeing the exhibits as she went. A skull scowled at her. She kept her back to the woman because she didn't want to give any clue of her intention to run as soon as she got to the door.

"Star…" The woman's voice in her ear. Amélie started. She hadn't heard her cross the gallery. "Where's your star?"

She spoke quietly, her voice soft. Amélie turned around. The woman put a hand on her shoulder.

"I can see the outline, did you take it off?"

Amélie ran. She brushed off the woman's hand and headed for the door. It was one of those big heavy ones that must be constructed in a special museum door factory.

Amélie shoved at it, all the time expecting the woman to grab her or raise the alarm.

She was through before either happened and out into the hall. She glanced back as she went out the main door and stood at the top of wide steps leading down to a square. Across the river the Tour Eiffel glinted in the autumn sunshine.

Her sense of relief that no-one followed her vanished as she took in the square. Four trucks, soldiers jumping from three of them – the fourth free for prisoners. The Germans knew the desperate used museums as daytime shelter. They'd come to catch their prey.

An officer shouted at his men as they lined up in front of the trucks for final orders before beginning the hunt.

Amélie spun round and, as calmly as she could, stepped back into the revolving door. She pushed hard and it spun her back into the vast hall. The entrance to the Musée de l'Homme was to her left and standing in its doorway was the woman.

Amélie froze. She waited for the woman's accusation. Instead she flicked her head – 'this way' – and went back into the museum. Amélie's mind raced, why hadn't she yelled the place down, why hadn't she dashed forward and seized Amélie for the Germans?

The sound of heavy boots on the steps outside hurried her through the museum door. The woman was waiting. She grabbed Amélie by the wrist.

"Come, quick," she said.

She led Amélie down a long corridor. They rushed past door after door.

"In here," said the woman. She opened a door and closed it behind them. "Round there, under the desk, hurry..."

Amélie did as she was told. They were in an office, a row of filing cabinets filled one wall, a couple of chairs and a table sat in front of a tall, thin window, in the middle was a table with a half-assembled skeleton on it and at the far end was a large desk with a solid front. Amélie scampered round behind, pulled out the chair and curled herself into the leg space beneath the desk. Thankfully the woman was not tall so when she sat on the chair and pulled it into the desk her legs did not squash Amélie.

There was a rustle of papers as she resumed her work.

"Shhh. Silence, not a sound, don't even breathe."

For a time, there was silence, apart from the sound of the woman writing, a peculiarly comforting scratching of pen on paper as she inked out grand, museum-worthy words.

The noise of boots coming down the corridor drowned out the scratching. Doors the length of the corridor were thrown open, followed by loud, angry commands and loud, angry replies. Footsteps stopped outside their door. The door was flung open.

"Ohhh," said the woman, alarm in her soft voice. "What is this? What's going on?"

"Ah, Mademoiselle," came the reply in heavily-accented French. "This is your office?"

Amélie could sense the room filling with men.

"Oui."

"You are alone here?"

"Oui, of course – I am at my work."

"Who are you?"

"Assistant curator."

"You are alone?"

"Oui."

"We will search the room."

"If you must, I really don't know what you're hoping to find."

"Jews, Mademoiselle, Jews and criminals… and anyone foolish enough to be sheltering them. Which is an offence punishable by death."

Footsteps approached until they were centimetres from Amélie, separated by the solid front of the desk. Amélie held her breath.

"You will remain seated, Mademoiselle – you must not interfere."

"Of course, Monsieur Capitaine."

Amélie made out the muffled sound of the scratch of the pen and the noise of cupboards being opened. Madamoiselle was a cool one resuming her work amid this German invasion of her office.

It did not take long. Amélie heard the captain click the heels of his boots together.

"Merci, Mademoiselle," he said. "We will find them elsewhere."

"Oh no you won't," said the woman quietly as the door slammed shut. Amélie wondered if Germans ever entered or left a room without slamming the door.

"Stay there," she whispered.

Amélie waited. Her legs began to protest about being curled up for so long. The Germans were still in the museum, she could hear shouts elsewhere and the tramp of endless boots up and down the corridor.

At last calm returned. That type of calm particular to a museum; curators and visitors lost in their own thoughts. Only this time everyone had only one thought. Have they gone?

There was a gentle tapping on the door, tap-tap, tap. Like a secret signal.

"Oui?" said the woman.

The door opened. "Clear," said a man's voice.

"Good," said the woman. "You can come out now."

"Ow, ow, ow…" Amélie hopped around the room trying to get the pins and needles out of her left leg.

The man and the woman laughed.

"It's not funny," growled Amélie.

"You look like a little bird, ma chérie," said the woman.

"A little bird with long legs," said the man. "A baby stork."

"Shhh, Alain, enough," instructed the woman. "Do not be unkind."

She was young, younger than Amélie expected someone working in a museum to be, with a smiley face beneath a high forehead and brown hair pulled back into a ponytail from which a number of strands had worked themselves loose.

"I must go," said Amélie and limped towards the door. The man, older and tall but with rounded shoulders and a slight stoop as if he was embarrassed about his height, stood aside.

"Where?" wondered the woman.

Amélie turned. "Thank you for what you did – it was… very brave, and kind. But I must go home."

"Home?"

"Oui."

"I don't think it is safe for you out there."

Amélie's hand was on the doorknob.

"It is not safe for Jewish people in Paris – you will be in great danger. I've seen you in the museum before… you are alone aren't you?"

Amélie shrugged. A tear rolled down her right cheek.

"We can hide you here…"

"Cécile!" interrupted the man.

She stood up from behind her desk and walked towards Amélie, arms outstretched.

"Shhh, Alain," countered Cécile. "We must. My little bird, stay… we will think of something. We have some of the cleverest people in Paris in this museum, so in all France – if we cannot think of something then France really is condemned forever to live under the Boche… oops."

Cécile put her hand over her mouth in mock regret. Amélie smiled and sniffed. Cécile put a hand on Amélie's arm.

"Will you stay?"

"Oui."

Chapter 8

She slept on a camp bed in the museum cellar. It was hidden in a corner behind a pile of boxes. Amélie hoped they didn't contain bones and skeletons and decided not to look just in case.

They left her with a candle, which gave a small circle of light, but when she blew it out the darkness folded itself around her and tucked her in. She fingered the key to the apartment, still on her mother's chain around her neck. Her last piece of home.

That first night, huddled under the blankets from head to toe, Amélie was frightened – not that she admitted it to Cécile when she arrived the next morning with breakfast, a stale chunk of baguette and gooseberry jam.

"My mother makes it," said Cécile, "sends it to me from the country. It makes even the hardest bread taste good.

"I have some clothes for you and a toothbrush, towel and soap – you can go up and use the bathroom before we open…"

"I was going to go home today and get my things," interrupted Amélie.

Cécile shook her head. "Too dangerous."

"But I want my…"

"Non," snapped Cécile. "I said it is too dangerous… this is life and death, Amélie… if you're caught we all suffer for it."

The day took a turn for the better once she was dressed. Cécile took her to help in the archive room. They were packing up some of the museum's exhibits to send to the south, away from the Germans. After France surrendered and the British army escaped from Dunkirk, the Germans divided the country – the north and west was ruled by the Germans, and the Gestapo, in the south a French government ruled. They did what the Germans wanted but it was a little safer. For the time being.

Amélie enjoyed having something to do, recording carefully where each bit of each exhibit went – you wouldn't want to waylay a skeleton's feet – and wrapping them in old newspaper.

"You could put me a box and smuggle me to the south," she said with a grin.

Cécile raised an eyebrow.

At night Amélie put her camp bed together – it had to be taken up and hidden each morning – and lay in the darkness wishing she at least had Champs-Élysées with her. She tried to think of Maman and Papa and Paulie as often as she could to make sure the pictures she carried in her head did not fade. Some mornings she woke up and remembered she hadn't thought of them before she went to sleep. Guilt slithered through her mind.

One night she couldn't sleep. Cécile had scolded her that afternoon for sitting outside on the steps in the autumn sunshine. Amélie knew she'd done wrong, put herself and others in danger, but she'd been so desperate for a moment of fresh air.

She sighed and threw off the blankets. She was used to the dark now. She opened the door and peeked out. The corridor outside was dark but not as pitch black as her 'bedroom'. Her eyes adjusted to this lighter darkness and looked left towards the stairs then right towards… she didn't know, she'd never been to the end of the corridor. It wasn't allowed.

She put a hand on the wall to help guide her. She tried

the next door. It was locked. The corridor turned to the right. At the far end a sliver of light showed beneath a door. There was a noise, the crank and grind of machinery, not loud but consistent.

She edged down the corridor and pressed an ear to the door. Still the sound. She knelt down to try and peer beneath the…

The door opened, someone came out and tripped over Amélie.

"Aaarrgghh," he yelped as he hit the ground.

"Alain!" An alarmed hiss from inside the room. Amélie knelt up – Alain had knocked her flat with his tumble. She pushed his feet aside, glanced up at another pair of legs and saw a pistol pointing at her. She could see into the steely blackness of its barrel, but not far enough to see the bullet.

"Get up," said the owner of the gun.

"Oww," groaned Alain. "My wrist."

"Quiet, Alain… you, get up."

Amélie stood up. She felt silly standing there in her nightshirt, a nightshirt too big for her – it was an old one of Cécile's. It made her look like a ghost from one of those horror movies Paulie liked so much.

"Amélie!"

Cécile joined the two men at the door. Alain was still on the floor groaning. Amélie had thought he was a fusser since that first day in Cécile's office. She picked up his glasses and handed them back to him.

"I… I… heard a noise… thought it might be burglars…"

"Burglars?"

"Come on, get her in – and him. Get this door closed, do you want to tell the whole world what we're doing." The stranger with the gun gestured at Alain.

Amélie stepped into the room and looked around.

"What are you doing?"

"Never you mind," snapped the stranger.

He was a tall with short, dark hair brushed back from his face. He had the look of a film star but villain rather than hero, a good boy gone bad.

"Shhh," he ordered. He walked out of the room, closing the door behind him.

"What…" began Amélie.

"Shh," hissed Cécile.

They waited in silence for him to return.

"All quiet," he said as he stepped back into the room. "Let's get it done – we can't waste any more time. You…" He gestured at Amélie with the gun… "you sit over there, we'll deal with you later. Now…"

"I saw the light," interrupted Amélie.

"Enough," barked the stranger.

"What light?"

"We don't have time for this, Cécile," said the man – everything he said sounded like an order.

Cécile ignored him.

"Amélie?"

"Beneath the door." She pointed. "Saw it as soon as I turned the corridor. The noise as well... you should put something over the door."

"Yes," said Cécile. "I see."

"Alain," ordered the stranger. "Pin a blanket over the door. Roll up another at the bottom. Quickly, get on with it..."

He returned to the machine occupying the middle of the room, cranked a handle, fiddled with a switch and it came to life.

"A printing press!" exclaimed Amélie.

He scowled at her. Cécile smiled. She leaned over and spoke into Amélie's ear, her hand covering her mouth so neither of the men could make out a word she was saying.

"You must remember the best men went off to the war – the ones we're left with, well..." Cécile shrugged, a gesture

58

that said everything. She grinned again. "We woman on the other hand – we have the best of France's women aiding the resistance against the damn Boche."

"You are the Resistance?"

"We are resisting the Germans, doing what we can. We are small but we will grow."

"What are you saying?" barked the stranger, raising his voice above the huffing and puffing of the printing press, an ancient machine that belonged where they were; in a museum.

"Later," said Cécile.

They watched the leaflets come off the press. Cécile handed one to Amélie to read. The ink was still wet and her fingertips were smudged black by the time she'd read both sides.

It was a call to arms – an article written by someone called The Axe, asking fellow citizens of France to resist the Germans in any way they could. "Do not make their occupation of our great land easy," they wrote. "It is not time yet to take to the barricades as our forefathers once did but that day will come and until then we must begin with small footsteps of RESISTANCE. Even reading my words is one."

They signed off with "Vive La France."

"Long live France," shouted Amélie as she turned over the leaflet. The other side had snippets of news from beyond France. Britain was holding out, there was fighting in the African desert, everywhere there was war. At the bottom was a recipe for a cake without having to use butter, which was all but impossible to get hold of in Paris. And a "Tip for surviving the Occupation." This one was for using straw and hay in punctured bicycle tyres – new tyres were also a rare find.

"We have to write something that isn't just war," said Cécile. "Something that might be useful."

The stranger turned off the press.

"This is Raymond," said Cécile. "He thinks he's in charge."

"I am in charge," said Raymond. "I'm sorry young lady you must find somewhere else to stay. Cécile will help you of course but this is no place for a child."

"She's a Jew," said Cécile. "If you send her from here you're sending her to her death."

"Nonsense," said Raymond. "It's too risky having her here – children won't win the war for us and if we don't win the war many more children will die. I'm sorry but she goes tonight. That's my final decision."

Raymond said all this without looking at Amélie. She

walked over to the press and picked up one of the bundle of leaflets Alain was wrapping in brown paper.

"You have to take these around Paris, don't you? It's no good if people don't read it."

"Obviously," said Raymond, "now please put those down, this doesn't concern you."

"I'll take it round Paris for you – help you," declared Amélie. She knew Cécile was right – if she left here, where would she go? She would not last out there with the Germans hunting high and low for anyone Jewish. After her escape her name was sure to be high on their 'Wanted' list. Besides here was a way for her to do what she'd sworn – fight the Germans. The Axe was right, begin little and little-by-little make a difference.

"Raymond," continued Amélie. Raymond looked startled that she was addressing him directly. "I know the streets of Paris, I know the back streets of Paris. Adults, French, German, all of you, you look through children, you don't see us.

"I can deliver your newspaper much easier than any of you – nobody will suspect me. And if I am caught…" This time it was Amélie's turn to shrug… "…what have you lost? Only a child and what does one child matter in this whole war across the world?"

Cécile winked at her. "Bravo," she said.

"No… I don't think…" began Raymond.

"She's right," interrupted Alain. "Remember, we've still to replace Yvonne." He turned to Amélie. "You realise how dangerous this is? If you're caught… being a child will not save you."

"I know," said Amélie. The thing was, she no longer felt a child. She still wanted to be one, because she liked being a child. She didn't want to grow up yet. Like Peter Pan in that English storybook of Maman's. But for the moment she would have to be something else, a resister, a fighter and once she'd helped win that fight – like Peter Pan against the Pirate – and got Maman and Papa and Paulie back she could be a child again.

"Do you?" said Raymond.

"Yes," said Amélie. "I will do this for you, for France."

"Bravo," said Cécile again.

"And," said Amélie, her voice dropping to a whisper as Raymond began to give instructions, "for Maman and Papa and Paulie."

Chapter 9

And so, overnight, Amélie Dreyfus joined a resistance group. Its youngest member and, who knows, quite possibly the youngest member of la résistance in the whole of France.

The way she saw it, back in her camp bed later that night, sleep a million miles away, she had no choice. She would have been out on the street if Raymond had his way, and when she was caught – because on her own she would be caught – that would mean Drancy, the camp in the north of the city where Jews were being collected, and then a train to the East. Nobody had heard of anybody coming back from the East. There were stories, awful stories… but they might just be stories. That's what she had to hold on to, for Maman and Papa and Paulie's sake, and for hers. In war it is difficult to find the truth.

Which was the first aim of the Musée Network. Tell the people of Paris the truth about the occupation. Cécile began instructing Amélie in her new life straight after breakfast the following morning.

First, the Network; Raymond led it, she and Alain helped write, print and distribute the newspaper – an act punishable by death if the Germans found out.

"They have spies everywhere – Gestapo agents and French people, traitors who work for them. Guard your tongue always, guard your trust," said Cécile. There were others in the Network who did other work, but she would not tell Amélie anymore. "It's dangerous to know – for you and them."

"Why?" said Amélie. She had so many questions and was trying ever so hard not to ask them.

Cécile glared at her. "Because if you are captured and the Gestapo torture you. You will have nothing to tell them beyond me, Alain and Raymond and the museum."

"I will never tell them anything," said Amélie. They sat in silence for a while.

"Does it hurt a lot?" said Amélie. Her voice wobbled.

"I should imagine so," said Cécile.

"Ah," said Amélie. She swallowed, then spoke slowly

to better control her voice. "I will be careful, always – I promise."

"And so do I," said Cécile and threw her arms around Amélie. She smelt nice; like a big sister might, thought Amélie.

For the rest of the day Cécile was more like a teacher. They sat in the archive room, surrounded by history, as Cécile talked her through becoming a courier for the Musée Network. Even though they were alone Cécile kept her voice low. "You never know who might be listening," she said.

Amélie was to become like one of those butcher's boys who peddle madcap through the streets to deliver their chops and chicken. Except her peddling had to be sedate, careful and, most of all, unnoticed.

"Do nothing to attract attention – become a ghost on the streets, a schoolgirl carrying her books home. An invisible.

"Go only where you're told to go, deliver only to the person you're told to deliver to. If they are not in, make a polite apology and leave. If you can't find an address never ask, move on to the next one."

On Cécile went listing the dos and lots and lots of don'ts. Use only the password when you make a delivery. If the person tries to talk to you, shake your head and move on.

"And finally, if you get caught up in a German

checkpoint, abandon the bike – and run. You, your life, is more important than a parcel of leaflets. Take no risks, do nothing more than make your deliveries – nothing more. Do you understand?"

Amélie nodded.

"Good." Cécile studied her face. "You sure you want to do this – if you're too scared don't worry I can find work for you here – I'll not have you thrown out, my darling."

"I'll do it."

"Very well," said Cécile, giving a slight nod of her own. "You must learn these."

She opened the folder in front of her and took out a piece of paper. "Learn these addresses – off by heart. I have a street map – we'll plan your route. Then we'll burn the paper. You must remember the addresses, contact names and your route. All in your head – never write any order or address or contact down. D'accord?"

"D'accord." Amélie looked at the paper. Ten addresses, ten names, just first names, Claude, Peter, Jean, Nina…

Cécile stood up. "You've half an hour before you must leave – it's best these things are done as fast as possible. I'll leave you to learn."

She leaned forward and placed a kiss on top of Amélie's head. "You're a brave girl."

Amélie said nothing.

"There is one more thing... we ask everyone this. It's not an order – it couldn't be. It doesn't matter that you are a child, I'll still ask it of you because... because you're one of us."

Amélie looked up. Her stomach felt tight.

"If – and I pray this will not happen – if you are taken we ask that you try and hold out for one day before talking..."

"I will never talk," said Amélie fiercely.

Cécile raised a hand. "Everyone talks eventually... everyone... just try and say nothing for a day. It gives us time to close up the network and get away before they come for us."

"Okay."

Cécile smiled. "When this is over, Amélie, I think we shall be the best of friends and walk down the Champs-Élysées arm-in-arm in the prettiest dresses in Paris."

"Okay," said Amélie, although she didn't feel at all okay.

Chapter 10

The bicycle wobbled as Amélie set off from the museum. It was a heavy bike, belonged to Yvonne, the previous courier. No-one mentioned where Yvonne was now and Amélie didn't ask. She didn't want to know.

For a moment she thought of stopping the bike, getting off and walking away. Only for a moment. She found her balance and was off, standing up to push hard on the pedals and picking up speed.

Within a couple of streets, she felt better. A couple more and a smile sneaked on to her face. It was good to feel the air on her face again, feel the sun warming her shoulders, and breathe the smells of her city. She caught the whiff of a bakery and raised her nose into the air like a dog. What a smell, even if most of it would end up in German stomachs.

She crossed the river, now in its autumn colours, grey

and greyer, and took a round-about route through the south of the city – just in case anyone had followed her from the museum. Once she stopped and fiddled with her tyre but saw no-one who looked like they might be a Gestapo spy.

The first address was the furthest away, near the Gare d'Austerlitz. This one, the home of a retired policeman, was the trickiest Cécile had warned because of being near to one of the city's busiest stations. Amélie found the address on the top of her list, now written in her mind, and trudged up to the third floor, bumping her bike up the wide staircase because she didn't dare leave it in the street in case anyone looked beneath the schoolbooks in the bike's basket.

She rang the bell. The door opened a crack, lending a little light to the dark landing.

"Monsieur Claude?"

"Oui"

"Bonjour – I am Amélie. The password is Marie Antoinette. I have a package for you from…"

"Yes, yes…" He lowered his voice. "Quick, give it to me and go."

The door slammed in Amélie's face as soon as she'd handed the brown-paper package over.

"Nice to meet you too," she said and bumped her bike all the way down again.

It was after dark by the time she returned to the museum. She was tired and feeling grumpy because of a late detour when she spotted a German checkpoint on the bridge she'd planned to cross.

"You're late…how was it?" wondered Cécile, who had been waiting by the back entrance to the museum. She took the bicycle from Amélie and stored it under the stairs.

Amélie shrugged. "One person was not in – the rest I gave out."

"Who?"

"Madame Lilly."

"Okay – I'll have that checked. Now, come I've saved some dinner."

She put an arm around Amélie's shoulders and squeezed. "You have done well."

"Have I? It doesn't feel like I've done anything."

Cécile stepped in front of Amélie and put a hand on each shoulder.

"My little bird, you have. It may not seem much but imagine all over France people like you doing little things and add them all together and you have a resistance. It is important what you do and it is brave. You'll feel better about it in the morning, you'll see."

Cécile was right. The next morning there was another

list to learn, another 10 names and addresses and another hour pouring over the map planning her route. This time she plotted a path using the smaller bridges over the river, hoping they were less likely to be patrolled by the Germans. She drew her route of the night before in pencil – she would do that after each trip to try and make sure she took a different path as often as possible. That way there was less chance of someone spotting her and becoming inquisitive.

She looked down the list of names.

"Madame Lilly?" she asked Cécile.

Cécile shook her head.

"What…" begun Amélie but Cécile shook her head again. Amélie had entered a world where questions were not welcome.

The outside world changed before her eyes as autumn stumbled into winter. People disappeared and she saw them go – lines of women and children with Yellow Stars on their coats herded along the streets. First they were taken to the Vélodrome d'Hiver, the winter velodrome, on the Boulevard de Grenelle and the smart people who lived in the tall houses lining the well-to-do street looked the other way. There was, so they assured each other, nothing they could do.

Some of the gendarmes who helped with the round-up were in tears. Still they shepherded their Jewish flocks into the velodrome. Amélie rode on, glancing at her left breast as she did, as if expecting her Star to reappear and reveal her to the watching German guards and their snarling dogs.

One night, Cécile told Amélie, the flock were taken from the velodrome to the station and hurried on to trains for the east, the barking of guard dogs, whimpers of children and growl of truck engines the only sounds in the darkness. A sharp whistle from the train sent a last farewell to their home city.

For much of Paris it was out of sight and out of mind. How could this be happening? The question nagged at Amélie. She asked Cécile. How? Cécile looked away. "I don't know," she said. Life went on.

Lines outside shops grew. Many women – and it was always the women – began queuing in the dark, especially if there were rumours of something extra on the way. This was a world where the smallest queue meant waiting half an hour for a bag of brussel sprouts – the 'devil's vegetable' Paulie called it, which made Amélie laugh. Imagine Paulie having to live on brussel sprouts. She liked remembering things her brother had said and done because it made her smile, kept Paulie, and Maman and Papa, alive in her head.

She proved good at what she had to do for the network. Even Raymond was pleased with her, though he never told her so. It was down to Cécile to pass on orders. And sometimes Amélie was given secret messages to deliver as well as the bundles of leaflets, brown paper packages, tied up with string and hidden beneath schoolbooks she'd never open.

Every night at a quarter past eight they would make their way to the attic and Cécile would set up the secret radio so they could tune into the BBC. For five minutes the BBC broadcast in French – *Les Français parlent aux Français* it was called, the French talking to the French – a mix of news and secret messages. "Message important… message important… Clarice has blue eyes… Clarice has blue eyes…"

All over France, Cécile explained, resistance groups were listening in secret waiting for a message to make sense to them. Just being caught listening meant prison, perhaps worse. One night the BBC declared that French citizens had a duty to paint V for Victory signs on walls across the country. "Shall we?" said Amélie, liking the sound of that.

"No, absolutely not. Everything we do must be a secret – our work is too important, we must do nothing to draw attention to ourselves."

The secret messages she delivered never made any sense at all to Amélie. "The pen of my aunt writes best with red ink and never runs out…" she would repeat through a half-open door. The recipient would nod, thank her and close the door. Amélie knew it was code but also knew she could never ask what it meant.

She didn't always get it right, especially at the beginning. Cécile scolded her for trying to talk to the people she delivered to, for introducing herself. "Tell no-one your name – no-one," she ordered.

Just to be sure they gave her a new name, her network name. So Amélie became Vette, Vette Santine and trained herself to answer to Vette and ignore Amélie – Amélie was packed away, like the precious belongings she'd placed in the suitcase beneath the bathroom floor at home.

They gave her new papers. Vette Santine they stated, with an address she'd never visited. Most important of all: there was no large J stamped on them. Her Jewishness went into the suitcase too. It would come out again one day, when Amélie did, but for now it must be hidden.

To help with the disguise Cécile gave her a school uniform. "You're sending me to school," said Amélie in horror when she was presented with the grey skirt and grey, red-lined blazer. "I will not go."

"Non, non," said Cécile and giggled. "Wear this for your deliveries – it's a Catholic school, where children of important people go, rich people, powerful people… it will hide you in plain sight."

It meant Ame… Vette had to learn to cross herself, just in case. Forehead, chest, left shoulder, right shoulder… up, down, left, right, up, down, left, right, up, down, left, right.

Cécile was right. The uniform, as well as the new identity papers, helped Vette out of tight corners. Once she cycled round a corner and nearly knocked over an officer manning a checkpoint. As he yelled for her papers and demanded his men search her, a gendarme whispered something in his ear and gestured at her uniform. The officer settled for a grumpy glance at her papers before waving her on.

The gendarme put a hand on her handlebars. "I suggest, Mademoiselle, you ride with a little more care," he said before letting go. Vette smiled at him and nodded, all the time her stomach doing somersaults.

She made one mistake. She hadn't thought it was a mistake. The network's newspaper called for all women to wear the colours of France on a certain day to show the nation's unbroken defiance of the Germans. So for her 'deliveries' that Saturday Vette found a red skirt, a white blouse and a blue scarf and beret.

She was cheered a couple of times on her rounds and waved back. She was beaming as she rode her bike back into the museum courtyard. Cécile, in her usual grey skirt and white blouse, hurried down the steps and pulled her inside, the bike falling to the cobbles with a crash.

"You idiot," she said and slapped Vette on the cheek. Vette pushed Cécile away. They eyed each other. Vette could see the anger in Cécile's eyes, felt the anger flaring inside her.

"Do you want to get us all caught…" Cécile's voice was hoarse, as though she was stopping herself from shouting at Vette.

"What? No… of course not…"

"You dress… dress like that…"

"But that's what the paper, our paper said…"

Vette's eyes pricked with tears.

"Non, non, non… you cannot do that, you cannot draw attention to yourself. We must stay in the shadows, always the shadows."

"I…" began Vette.

Cécile let out a sudden sob. It seemed to take her as much by surprise as it did Vette.

"I'm sorry," she said. "But you…"

"I'm sorry as well. It won't happen again."

"I'm tired," said Cécile. "So tired. Every day, worrying, being careful, oh so careful, so much to remember…"

She opened her arms and Vette stepped into them.

"I will become a shadow…" she mumbled into Cécile's shoulder. "No-one will see me come and go – I will live in the shadows."

Cécile sniffed and then spoke in a whisper. "Every day I expect them to come for me, every day I expect you not to come home. Stay in the shadows, my little bird, stay in the shadows."

Chapter 11

The early winter sun was shining on Amélie's front door. Across the street, in the shade, Vette stopped her bike. She looked up to the third floor. There was no sign of life in the Dreyfus apartment. The exterior's faded green paint – as long as she could remember it had been faded – looked a little more tired, a little more chipped. She wanted to go up but knew she wouldn't. She would stay here in the shade.

Vette felt pleased with herself. She'd recognised the address, the ninth on her list for the day. The best way to get there was by going down her street. It would allow her to have a look at the apartment, only a look and she would resist the temptation to go in no matter how loudly home called her.

She granted herself a little smile. It froze on her face

when she saw the sign. It was on the right of the front door to the block, red writing on a blue background.

"No Jews."

"Huh," she said, stood up in the saddle and pushed down on the pedal. It did not take long to find the address, deliver the message and pedal briskly back to the museum.

The sun had already given way to the gloominess of a winter's evening by the time she pushed her bike into the courtyard. She knew every inch of the museum now, where everything was kept and it didn't take her long to find what she wanted. She lifted the schoolbooks out of her basket and replaced them with her finds.

If she hurried she could be there and back before curfew – provided she had the luck of an empty street when she needed it.

She did. She left the bike down a nearby alley and carried what she needed into her street. The front door was shut – in winter the concierge always closed it as soon as darkness arrived, bolted it too so any resident had to ring the bell and take a ticking off when she shuffled across the courtyard to open it.

A glance up and down the street and she began. She dipped the brush into the pot and swept it down the wall, a sprinkle of paint drops patterned her skirt. 'NO,' she painted as large as she could, "BOCHE." Right over the sign. And then, just for good measure and because she still had plenty of paint, she slapped a large 'V' on the door.

She took the skull – a scary looking thing 'borrowed' for a greater good from one of the stored boxes in the museum – and placed it carefully on the front doorstep.

"That's for Amélie," she said, checked the coast was clear and hurried to her bike.

Vette was back at the museum in no time, well before curfew. She poked her head around the door to Cécile's office to say good night – Cécile often slept on a camp bed in the museum because it was warmer than her own rented room in a chilly apartment.

"All okay, my darling," said Cécile. She looked tired, black bags beneath her eyes.

"Oui, oui," said Vette in her breeziest voice.

"What's that on your hand?"

Vette looked at her paint-stained fingers. "Oh, nothing... wet paint, on a door, pushed at it to open it... silly me. Good night, Cécile."

In the morning she was sitting on her bed dabbing at her skirt with a wet towel – the paint marks were worse than she'd thought – when Cécile came in. She looked more anxious with every new day.

"Come," she said. "Quick."

As they walked down the corridor and hurried up the stairs to the top floor, Cécile glanced down at Vette's skirt. She knows, thought Vette.

"I know," said Cécile, "you'll be wondering why we're coming up here…"

"I wasn't," said Vette.

"Really?" said Cécile and opened the first door they came to on the top floor.

"Um, yes," said Vette stepping into a large room. Shelves packed with books and manuscripts lined the walls. A long, narrow table ran down the middle. Raymond was sitting at the far end. He had his head in his hands.

"Raymond?" said Cécile.

He glanced up. "Pardon, I was a long way away."

"Somewhere nice I hope," said Cécile and smiled at him. When she smiled the worry lines on her face disappeared.

"No," he said. "Sit down."

Cécile pulled out a chair and beckoned for Vette to be seated. She stood behind.

"Odd," said Raymond, staring out the window. "A skull was found outside a house last night up behind Montmartre – a gendarme was just here asking if it was ours. I rather think it was but said not."

He looked at Cécile. "Know anything about that?"

Cécile shook her head.

"Huummm," he said, his brow furrowing. "The last thing we need is gendarmes poking their noses around here... perhaps it is linked..."

"To what..." Vette couldn't hold her tongue any longer. Raymond looked at her for the first time, as if surprised to see her there.

"There is a traitor," he said, stood up and crossed to the window.

"Is that why I'm here... I, I just painted over the sign, to give a sign to them... I'm not a..."

"Paint?" said Raymond turning around. "What paint? Enough, we've no time for this."

He returned to his seat and leaned forward, elbows on the table.

"I accept you were right, Vette Santine – children can be unseen, can come and go beneath the noses of the Boche." He nodded his head at her, a reluctant apology. "Which is why we need you to do something for us as a matter of urgency..."

"What?" said Vette.

"It's dangerous, very dangerous but it might, just might save some of the network."

"I'll do it," said Vette without hesitation. She hadn't felt scared at all in recent weeks. Maybe Vette didn't get scared, maybe she'd left all her fear in Amélie.

"Very well," said Raymond. He glanced at Cécile, who took a folded piece of paper from her pocket and placed it on the table in front of Vette. "So we have a traitor…"

"Who?"

Raymond shrugged. "I suspect it is Alain…"

"Alain!"

"Probably but that is not important now – there is a traitor and we must close down the network, as quickly as possible, all sections of it. We need you to go to those addresses – memorise them and destroy the paper before you go – check them, see if the Boche are on to us."

"What are they?"

"Safe houses – we… should I tell her?"

His question was aimed at Cécile.

"Yes," she said and put a hand on Vette's shoulder. "I trust her with my life."

"These are places we hide pilots, British pilots who've been shot down. Hide them until we can smuggle them down to the coast on one of our escape routes. There a boat meets them and they're taken back to England.

"We need to know if these houses have been discovered

83

– are they safe? They must be warned. You must be very, very careful, the Gestapo will be on the lookout for someone doing exactly this. You'll be taking your life in your hands. Do you understand?"

Vette nodded.

"Good, you are a brave girl. Fast as you can."

As they walked back down the stairs, Cécile stopped on the first landing. "You don't have to do this, you know?"

"I know."

Cécile repeated herself half-an-hour later in the courtyard. Vette had wolfed down her breakfast while staring at the piece of paper, willing the addresses to stick in her mind.

"Take this," said Cécile, wrapping a long woollen scarf around Vette's neck. "If you're not wrapped up against the cold you will stand out."

She kept her hands on the handlebars of the bike as Vette swung her leg over.

"You don't…"

"I do, Cécile, but I do – someone has to and I am the best person to do it."

They smiled at each other, thin lipped, determined smiles.

"Au revoir," said Cécile.

"Goodbye," said Vette and pedalled quickly out of the

courtyard. She heard the gate clank shut behind her and the slither of a bolt being pushed into place. She'd never known the gate to be bolted before.

It would take her, she reckoned about 15 minutes to make the first address as long as she didn't run into any patrols. She tucked her chin into the scarf and turned right at the end of the alley.

"Allez," she said to herself and pushed down hard on the pedal.

Chapter 12

Vette stopped around the corner from the first address. She needed a moment. She climbed off the bike and fiddled with her laces. Should she leave the bike and walk past? That would give her more time to study the safe house. But if there was something wrong she needed to get away as fast as possible.

She pulled the bike off the wall. "Courage, Amélie, courage," she whispered.

The street was quiet. A woman was walking down the far pavement. She went straight past the address and her head never turned. So there was probably nothing unusual to be seen. Vette cycled slowly down the street, glancing from left to right as though looking for a house number. She got a good look at 43; nothing out of the ordinary, shutters still drawn upstairs, open downstairs, the downstairs window open a little. No obvious sign of life, no obvious sign of the Boche.

Vette breathed out slowly as she reached the end of the street. She left her bike, walked back and knocked on the door, knots in her stomach. A woman opened it a crack. "You must leave," said Vette. "They know." She added the password. The woman nodded and closed the door. One done – five to go.

The next one was nearby and looked much the same – this time a boy answered and Amélie had to wait until he fetched his mother – the next was a little further but still nothing to set alarm bells ringing. Unlike the next one.

It was off the Rue Bichat, down an alley that lead towards the St Martin canal, an area of the city that had seen better days which meant it saw few Germans, the ideal location for a safe house.

There was a soft drizzle in the air, coating the neighbourhood in glumness. Vette turned her bike into the alley and tightened her grip on the handlebars. The alley was cobbled which made the bike shudder and jolt. But that wasn't the reason she held on so tight.

There was a man standing in a doorway about two-thirds of the way down. He was wearing a broad-brimmed hat and a long leather coat – the unofficial uniform of the Gestapo.

Vette glanced at the nearest door, number seven. That meant the address she was looking for would be halfway down.

She breathed a sigh of relief only for an urgent thought to check it. Of course the man wouldn't stand outside the actual door, he'd be on the lookout for anyone showing interest in the house or, even better, going in.

She started to half whistle, half whisper, 'Sur Le Pont d'Avignon', the song Papa used to sing in his warbly voice to get Amélie to sleep. He didn't know all the words so he used to make bits up.

"On the bridge at Avignon..."

He might not be Gestapo, he might be a man, just a normal man.

"All the world are dancing, prancing..."

No, he was Gestapo, every instinct in Vette's body was screaming it.

"On the bridge at Avignon..."

She began to pedal faster, still singing, still trying to look like a schoolgirl late for school. Only no schoolchildren round here wore uniforms like the one she had on.

"Time to cycle quicker, quicker..."

She risked a glance at number 33, taking in an open door hanging oddly, like someone had booted it open. A hatless man stepped out of it.

Her head turned as she cycled on. The hatless man came down the steps of the house, on to the cobbles. He had a gun in his hand.

"Her," he yelled, "seize her!"

But the cobbles were wet from the drizzle and he slipped, thudding down on to the hard surface of the alley. The gun clattered across the cobbles, as if continuing the pursuit of Vette.

She hunched over the handlebars and pushed hard on the pedals. The other leather-coat was stepping out of the doorway ahead of her, raising an arm, palm outstretched.

"Halt!" he snarled and realised too late Vette had no intention of obeying. The bike, old and heavy, helped her. She'd got it going now, the slope of the alley in her favour as she flew towards the Gestapo officer. He lowered his hand, looking to try and grab the handlebars, or failing that her.

Vette turned the front wheel so it was aimed just to the man's right and as she reached him raised her right foot and kicked out at him. His hands brushed the handlebars and fluttered along her arms. Her shoe caught him and the slithery cobbles came to her aid again. He fell backwards and she was past.

She shot out the bottom of the alley and on to the road

that led along the canal, mounted the far pavement and, just before hitting the railings along the canal bank, wrenched the handlebars to the right.

Vette and the bike skidded along the ground, the front wheel hung over the drop to the canal only for the handlebars to catch the bottom railing and prevent bike and rider from a soaking.

The pavement scraped her right leg, her tights tore and she gasped in pain. For a moment she lay there, on her side, legs and arms tangled with wheels, pedals and handlebars.

"Here, let me help you."

A boy, a little older than her, reached out a hand, pulled her up and grabbed the bike before it could slip into the oily waters of the canal. He looked at it carefully.

"You can ride it but it needs a...."

"HALT!" The cry came from the alley.

"You?" asked the boy, a puzzled look on his face. "But you're just a..."

"Merci," said Vette, grabbed the bike, gave it a push, put a foot on the pedal and swung a leg over. She could feel a warm trickle of blood sliding down her wounded thigh. She rode faster than she'd ever ridden. To the bottom of the street, then right over the canal bridge. There was another shout from one of the leather-coats. She didn't look back.

She hoped the boy wouldn't get in trouble for helping her – surely they would realise he was just a boy.

She laughed at the thought, a sudden moment of joy flooding through her. He was just a boy and she was just a girl... a girl who'd got away from the Gestapo. She turned again, heading towards the river; there was a bridge near here, a less busy one. Get over that and she knew a back-street route nearly all the way to the museum.

She slowed the bike, not wanting to attract any attention, and glanced down at her right leg. Her skirt had a dirty streak down it to add to the splotches of black paint. But at least it covered her ripped tights and bloodied thigh.

She stopped short of the bridge. There was no sign of any Germans or gendarmes. Her thigh stung. The thrill of her escape was draining away. She felt tired and sore, and then she remembered she hadn't finished – she still had one address to check.

She swung around and headed for the final house. Before she got there, she turned down another alley, lent her bike against the wall and crouched down, wrapping her arms tight around herself.

She squatted for a time, hugging herself. She wanted, really wanted to get back on her bike and cycle home, ride back to the apartment, climb to the third floor and hide herself in Maman's wardrobe where nobody would find her.

Except she knew she couldn't. She had people relying on her to complete her mission – if she didn't finish checking the houses, someone else would have to come out and they might not escape.

She winced as she stood up. Her leg hurt. She wheeled the bike back into the main street and 10 minutes later she was cycling up to the last address. This one was an apartment not unlike her own. She leaned the bike against a tree on the other side of the road, pulled at her necklace and kissed the key for luck. She slipped it back beneath her scarf and walked through the main door as if she lived there.

An old woman, the concierge, looked up from a large armchair that filled the doorway to the ground floor apartment.

"Bonjour," said Vette as breezily as she could. "Number Eight."

"Oui, oui," said the old woman, pausing from her knitting to offer a brief smile.

The stairwell was gloomy. Vette climbed swiftly, the busy clack of the woman's knitting needles marking time.

There were two apartments on each floor. The one she wanted was on the fourth. The door was ajar, a spill of light trickling into the landing. She pressed herself against the wall. Was it a trap? She listened. Not a sound.

Vette edged towards the door and listened again. Still nothing. She pushed the door, it swung open. The sound of a car starting in the street outside made her jump. She caught her breath and stepped into the small hallway.

There was a window at the far end. On the left-hand side two doors, both closed; on the right, one, open. She slid along the wall towards the open door. A cough brought her to an abrupt halt.

Vette froze. It came from the room belonging to the open door. A trap, it had to be a trap. She started to make her way back to the front door.

"I wonder how long he'll be – feels damned odd sitting out like this." Vette froze once more. Her mind raced. How long will who be? Sitting out like what? Hang on, never mind the who and the what… they were speaking English.

She stepped into the doorway. "Hello," she said.

"What the…"

Two men leapt up from armchairs placed either side of a fireplace in which a small blaze tried its hardest to warm the room.

"Who are you?"

"It's just a schoolgirl…" That came from the younger man. He looked young, wouldn't have appeared out of place in the boy's equivalent of her school uniform. He took a step towards her.

"Careful," suggested the other man, older and with a pencil-thin moustache neatly covering his top lip. His dark hair was brushed back into its precise place. He was small but stocky, everything about him was neat and tidy, unlike his younger companion, whose hair poked up all over the place. "Don't alarm her."

"I am not alarmed," answered Vette, in English. "Why are you talking in English – do you want to get yourselves captured?"

"I beg your pardon," said the older man.

"Are you idiots?"

"I beg your pardon," spluttered the older man.

"How dare you?" said the younger man.

Vette ignored them, spun on her heel and returned to the front door. She glanced out on to the landing.

"What…" The younger man had followed her.

"Shhh!" ordered Vette, raising a finger to her lips. "Stay there."

She tiptoed out into the darkness of the landing and

peeked over the balcony. She stood for a second and listened… nothing.

Back inside the apartment she closed the door as quietly as she could.

"I…" began the younger man.

"Non," hissed Vette. She took him by the arm and marched him back into the room. The man was so shocked he made no effort to resist. Once inside she closed the door and turned on the men.

"Parlez-vous français?"

The men looked blankly at her. She switched back to English, lowering her voice to little more than a whisper.

"You are stupid, sitting here, the apartment door open, talking in English like you are on holiday on the beach – you might as well invite the Gestapo to come in and get you. Stupid men… you stupid, stupid men…"

Vette stopped. She was losing control. The men were staring at her, both of them open-mouthed. She took a breath. She had to take control.

"I am from the network. I have to ask some questions… keep your voices down and please answer as simply as you can. Okay?"

The older man nodded. "I'm Wingfield-Hayes, this is…," he said.

"I don't need your names. Call me Vette. Who are you waiting for?" She had to put the pieces of the jigsaw together, and in a hurry.

"Why, Alan. Good chap, said he was off to fetch some chap who would take us to the coast, get us back to Blighty."

"Alain?"

"Yes, that's the one, glasses, stoop, get blown over in a stiff breeze…"

"We have to leave."

"What?"

"You… we are in danger, great danger."

She looked at the men. They looked back at her, expressions blank, waiting for her – for her – to tell them what to do.

"You must…" she began. "You must…"

She wasn't at all sure what they must do. First things first, Vette, she ordered herself.

"We must get out. Do exactly as I say – exactly. I will go first…" yes, now it was coming to her "… watch out the window in the hallway, it looks over la rue… how do you say? Ah yes, the street… look for me – I will cross the street to my bicycle. If I bend down to check the wheel, that is the sign for all clear and you come down. There is a concierge, best nod to her but do not talk. Come into the street and I

96

will walk with my bicycle. You stay behind me, 10 paces say, no make it 20, not together, you..." she pointed at the older man... "then another 10 paces and you..." a point at the younger... "Don't look at anyone apart from me or him. If I am stopped by the Boche or a policeman go, you're on your own. Don't come back here, it is not safe. Okay?"

"Yes," said the younger man.

"One question," said Wingfield-Hayes. "You said what you'll do if it's all clear... what will you do if it isn't safe for us to come down?"

Vette thought for a moment. "I will get on my bicycle and ride away."

"What about us?"

"Then you will be on your own."

Chapter 13

After the gloom of the stairwell, the light of the street made Vette blink. The drizzle had gone, replaced by weak winter sunshine. That was good for her plan, more reason for someone to be out for a stroll in the park.

She looked both ways as she crossed the street. As a sensible schoolgirl would. Her head was pounding, it was difficult to think. She looked both ways again – a cautious, sensible schoolgirl. She saw nothing so crossed the road.

If the Gestapo were not already here, somewhere, watching, they would be coming. She had to get the airmen out as soon as possible and get back to the museum to warn Cécile and Raymond.

She had her plan to get the airmen away but if it came to saving the airmen or getting back to the museum there was only one choice. She had to save Cécile. Cécile had saved her. If Cécile was taken by the Gestapo that was a death sentence.

She reached her bike, looked both ways again. Still nothing. She bent down and fiddled with the wheel, glancing up as she did so. There was a face in the fourth-floor window. She nodded.

It didn't take them long to emerge. Vette set off, pushing her bike. The first part of the route was the most dangerous because it was the busiest, after that she would take a series of back streets until they reached the park.

She looked back once to check the pilots were following as instructed then scanned the street ahead of her. Nothing. "Thank you," she muttered.

It took half an hour to make the park but felt a lot longer. Vette sat down on a bench and felt the energy drain from her. She was exhausted.

She waited for the men. For a moment she thought they weren't going to make it and for a moment she felt a weight lifted from her shoulders. If they'd been taken they weren't her problem anymore. Then she saw Wingfield-Hayes step through the gate into the park and look around, and her first thought was guilt. It was her job to save them. The younger man soon followed.

"Wait here," she said. "I'll go fetch help. Keep walking

around the park – it shouldn't be busy, you should be safe for a while."

The men nodded in turn. As she left the park she turned back. They were standing side-by-side watching her go. She pushed her bike and swung herself into the saddle and pedalled hard for the museum.

She went in the back way as usual. It was quiet inside. She made first for Cécile's office. The door was open a crack. She lifted her right hand to push it open and froze as she heard voices.

First Cécile. "Oh, I don't know who is in yet – nobody I think, not sure Raymond was even planning to come in today. He has a trip to take I think…"

Her voice sounded different, pretending.

"A trip… I don't know about any trip – why wasn't I told. What about the Jewish girl – she here?"

A man's voice, a voice Vette recognised.

"No, Alain, no I think she is out too. Why do you want to know?"

Alain here in the museum. Vette glanced up and down the corridor. If he was here then were the Gestapo too?

She stepped away from the door and tiptoed down the corridor. Once at the staircase she sprinted up the stairs, leaping two at a time. A listen at the door where she and Cécile met Raymond that morning. The room was empty.

Vette bolted back down the stairs, trying to be as mouse-like as she could, all the way to the basement. She found Raymond in the printing room. He was trying to dismantle the printing press. One of the pieces looked broken. There was a streak of ink across his face. He scrabbled in his pocket and pointed a pistol at her as she burst breathlessly through the door.

"Vette!"

"It's Alain… it is Alain…"

Raymond stepped towards her and caught her as she tripped over a metal plate taken from the press. He put her back on her feet.

"Pilots… English pilots, the park but Alain, Alain's here… upstairs. Gestapo…"

"Alain? Pilots, what pilots – where from?"

"England…"

"Yes, I know that, I mean… listen, take a breath, tell me what's happened."

Vette unscrambled her story, explaining how she'd left the pilots in the park and that she'd found the traitor. "Alain – he's upstairs, in Cécile's office. He's the…"

"I know – I didn't know he was here already." He glanced

round at the printing press. "We'll have to leave it… come, we're getting out."

Raymond took her by the hand and led her to the door.

"But," said Vette, pulling her hand lose. "Cécile, what about Cécile?"

"We can't… we have to…"

Vette shook her head. "We can't… I will not leave her."

Raymond stared at her. "Very well," he said. "But you're on your own. I have to make a telephone call, alert others – we cannot risk the entire network. The pilots are still in the park, right?"

She nodded. He glanced at his watch. "You have until one o'clock – I will see you in the park. If you are not there…" He shrugged. Vette nodded.

"Here," he added, "take this."

He handed the pistol to Vette. "Do you know how to use it?"

She shook her head. It felt heavy in her hand. "Well, pointing it is usually enough." He smiled at her. "Bonne chance, Vette."

She watched him hurry down the back stairs, took a deep breath and turned down the corridor to Cécile's office. She did not have long. There was nothing else to do but go on the attack. She pushed the door open and stepped in.

Cécile looked up from her desk. "Non," she said, standing up. Alain was by the large window, as if watching out for someone.

"Oh, it's you," he said, turning round.

Vette lifted her right arm and pointed the pistol at him. He seemed puzzled. She stared at Alain, her fear of him pulsing through her, and saw his confusion replaced by the look of a man even more scared than her.

"Sit down," said Vette, gesturing with the pistol. She tried to make her voice hard, as if she knew precisely what she was doing. Pale faced, Alain did as he was told. Vette crossed to the windows, grateful the size of Cécile's office allowed her to keep a distance between her and Alain.

The curtains were held open by two long ties. She tugged at them and the room turned to twilight, enough to see but none to spare.

She gave the ties to Cécile, who wrapped them around Alain's arms and legs to secure him to the chair.

"The Gestapo will be here any moment," he said. "They are on to us. We've been betrayed… someone…" Vette could tell he too was trying to make his voice hard. She said nothing, neither did Cécile. They left the room.

"DON'T LEAVE ME HERE," yelled Alain as they closed the door. "WE'VE BEEN BETRAYED."

In the corridor Vette flung her arms around Cécile.

"Careful," said Cécile as she felt the pistol still in Vette's hands.

"Oh, sorry," said Vette. Cécile took the gun and opened it with hands that knew what they were doing.

"It's not loaded," she said. "Did you know?"

"No," said Vette and giggled. She couldn't help herself.

Cécile smiled back. "Thank you," she said.

Chapter 14

Vette squealed and tried to tug her arm out of the man's tight grip. He'd emerged from thin air.

"Shhh," said Raymond. "It's me. Walk, don't look back. Cécile come."

He led them along the pavement away from the park gate. Neither of them had seen him coming, their attention all on the bench they could see beyond the gates.

The pavement followed the park railings. A curtain of trees and bushes in threadbare autumn costumes parted now and then to offer a view into the park.

"Where…" began Vette.

"No," snapped Raymond, "just walk."

"The pilots…"

Raymond tightened his grip on her elbow and increased his pace. He was hurting her.

"Okay, okay, I get it."

They crossed the street to a café. Raymond led them inside and nodded to the woman behind the counter. They took a table in the window.

"Coffees," said Raymond, holding up three fingers to remove any doubt.

"I don't…" began Vette.

"Do you ever shut up?" said Raymond. "Look." He directed one finger out the window.

There was a clear view across the park. They could see the bench. Two men were sitting on it, backs to the café.

"The pilots," said Vette. Raymond and Cécile glared at her as the café owner put down three cups of chestnut coffee – few places served real coffee anymore. Vette held her tongue.

They sat in silence and watched. One of the pilots, the younger one, glanced suddenly to his left. A man was walking towards the bench. He lifted his hand and pointed at the pilots.

The young pilot leapt to his feet. The man shouted something. Inside the café they could not make out the words. The young pilot started running. Two other men appeared from behind the trees on the far side to cut him off. Both pointed pistols at him. He raised his hands.

Wingfield-Hayes remained on the bench, his hands also in the air thanks to the first man directing a pistol at him.

Vette gripped the edge of her chair. There was a roaring in her ears. If she didn't hold on tight she would run. The tinkle of a handful of coins dropping on the tabletop startled her.

"Let's go," said Raymond.

They walked for a long while, east, into a neighbourhood Vette did not know. Raymond strode ahead, she and Cécile kept 20 paces behind, arms linked. It was only Cécile's support, Vette thought, that was keeping her going.

At last Raymond led them into another café, through a door in the back, across a small yard and up a rickety flight of stairs. He needed a shove of his shoulder to open the door at the top. It scraped over an uneven wooden floor, revealing an attic room, with a large bed at the far end and an ornate sofa at its foot. It looked like they'd stepped back in time.

"We stay here tonight – you two have the bed, I'll take the sofa. I'll get some food. Wait here."

What Raymond brought back, Vette never knew. She collapsed on to the bed, pulled her legs up to her chest and shut her eyes. They were taken. Might be dead. Because of her. Blood on her hands.

"You did all you could." Cécile sat on the bed. She stroked

the hair off Amélie's face, tucking it behind her ear. "It was not your fault, my little bird, not your fault. This is what happens. You must not blame yourself – it's not your fault."

Amélie wrapped her arms tighter around her legs, making herself as small as possible.

"Not your fault, not your fault, not your fault."

Cécile's voice rocked her to sleep.

When she woke she was beneath the covers. Sunlight streamed through the shutterless windows. Cécile lay next to her, on top of the covers. She could hear snoring. Raymond had pushed the sofa across the door and his large frame sprawled across it.

She rolled onto her side and pushed her hands between her knees to warm them. They'd felt cold since the café, since gripping the seat as if she were clinging to her life. There was the sound of a truck outside. Vette leapt from the bed and hurried to the window. It wasn't German as she'd feared, picturing grey helmets piling out of the back, heavy boots on the stairs.

"It's all right – we're safe here." Cécile was sitting up in the bed. She undid her plait and ran a hand through her hair.

"For the time being." Raymond spoke without opening his eyes.

Vette sat down on the window seat and stared into the street. A man in a wide cap was unloading crates from the back of the lorry. It was heavy work. She could see his breath in the chill morning air.

"What about Alain?"

"He doesn't know this place. Only I knew this place," said Raymond. He pushed himself upright and rubbed his face as if trying to warm it. It was cold in the room. Vette blew on the window panes and wrote her name, A-m-e-l-i-e, then rubbed it out with her sleeve.

"Couldn't we have saved them? Couldn't you have got them away? How did the Gestapo know where to find them?" She didn't look at Raymond. She was scared of what he might answer.

"You must have been followed," he said, "from the pilots' apartment…"

"But I checked."

Raymond looked at her. "These are people who've been doing this a lot longer than you, girl."

"Raymond," cautioned Cécile.

"Okay, okay… sorry – you did your best, Vette…"

"Raymond…" snapped Cécile.

"All right – you did well, Vette."

"I don't need you to give me a good report to take home – I'm not a schoolgirl."

Raymond stood up. "Yes you bloody well are – you're a girl. It's just as I said, children get in the way, mess things up – this is not playtime."

"I know…" Vette hissed. "I know, I messed up… I messed up, I don't know what else I could have done. You didn't tell me what I was supposed to do and it… it…" A cry of despair escaped before she could catch it.

Raymond looked surprised. He sat back on the sofa. "By god, I'm tired… I could sleep until the end of the war." He tipped his head back.

"I…" he said. "I'm sorry." He looked up at Vette. "Okay?"

She glared at him. He couldn't make it better; neither could Cécile.

"What do we do?"

Raymond shrugged. "We move on. It's done – you can't look back." He shrugged again. "It's war."

Chapter 15

The network, declared Raymond, was finished.

"We have to close it down – all of it, right away, save what we can but taking no, and I mean no…" and here he pointed a finger at Vette… "…no risks. Do I make myself clear?"

Vette nodded.

So what was left to save? Not much it turned out. But something. There were a couple of long-distance couriers who took pilots down the escape routes, either to the coast in Brittany or all the way down France, through the Pyrenees and over the mountains into Spain. They were both somewhere en route – if they hadn't been taken by the Gestapo. They would have to be warned off, told not to come back.

There were, revealed Raymond, three pilots left, one in

Paris, the other two just outside in a small village in a safe house unknown to Alain.

"We must save them – we must," said Vette. "We owe…"

"Yes, of course," said Raymond, frowning at the interruption. "But before we take them down the routes we must be sure – absolutely sure – they are who they say they are."

"What do you mean?"

"We need to be sure they're British…"

"Who else could they be?"

"Spies – the Gestapo have tried it before. A way to break into our escape routes. So we test pilots when they arrive with us – how do you speak English?"

"Maman, my mother… she was… is, she is English."

"Good, then we need you to do this – test their English, think of questions only a true Englishman would know. Can you do this?"

"Yes," said Vette, wondering whether she could.

She wondered some more on the way. She was following Raymond, 20 paces behind. Cécile had another job to do – they wouldn't tell Vette what. She hugged her tightly when they said goodbye.

"Listen," whispered Cécile into her ear after Raymond set off. "There is one other way out – just in case. Just for you – tell no-one understand, no-one. Annemasse, look on the map, near Geneva, on the border with Switzerland. My brother, Arnaud… Arnaud Tillion, he lives there. He will see you safe. Annemasse – remember Arnaud and Annemasse."

"I will see you again, won't I?"

Cécile hesitated. "Um, yes… yes, I hope so. Take great care, my little bird."

The pilot was a pale, broad-shouldered young man with a hunted look fixed on his face. He was shown into the kitchen of the small factory worker's house where he was hidden.

"Please," said Raymond, pointing at a chair on the other side of the table from Vette.

"Please," said Vette, "just answer my questions straight away, we only want your answers, nothing else."

"Very well," muttered the pilot. He crossed his arms and studied the table. When Vette asked her first question he looked up at her, puzzled.

"I beg your pardon," he said.

"What do children like doing best on the beach?" Vette repeated the question – Grandfather had always insisted you can spot a British child at the seaside because the first thing they do is make a sandcastle. "It's in our blood," Grandfather liked to announce. "Because an Englishman's home…" "Oui, oui, Grandpere," Amélie would reply and run away laughing chased, rather slowly, by a pretend-cross Grandfather.

"Well, building sandcastles probably," said the pilot. A small smile accompanied his answer as if he were seeing himself back on the beach as a child, before all this…

"And what is an Englishman's home?"

"His castle, I should rather think."

The pilot looked from Vette to Raymond. "Why's the girl asking me such silly questions?"

Raymond nodded him back to Vette.

"Just one more, sir… what did your father call the Germans in the Great War?"

"The Hun, the bloody Hun… look I don't…"

Vette glanced at Raymond and nodded. Raymond stood up. "Please wait here," he said in stuttering English.

Vette followed him into the corridor.

"Well?" said Raymond.

"I think he's English – as far as I can tell."

"Okay, good… listen there is more bad news – one of the couriers, she has gone, the other… we're not sure. So I have to ask you to do more. We must get the pilots away. Me and Cécile, we'll take two down to the Pyrenees. You, Vette, you must take this one to the coast."

"Me?"

"Yes. I can ask no-one else. I wouldn't ask if there was a grown-up who could do it…"

"I will do it." Vette nodded a full stop. No time to stop, no time to dwell.

"Good," said Raymond. "Here."

He handed her a piece of paper with two names on it, a man and a station. She read it through; meet a man outside a station far from here. Then she would be in the hands of another network. She was getting good at memorising names and addresses. It was like she was taking a photograph with her mind. She crumpled up the paper and looked around. There was no fire. She popped it in her mouth, chewed a couple of times, held her nose and swallowed.

"Good," repeated Raymond. "But first before you leave Paris you must go to Café de Biarritz, a man, call him Jo le Boxeur, will meet you. You have the password. He will give you papers for the pilot and a travel permit for you both, oh and the tickets. Your permit will not be in your name, short notice you see, so… well, that's up to you."

He put out his hand. "Bonne chance."

Vette shook his hand. "Good luck to you too."

Raymond put his hand on the door and paused. "It is likely they will be waiting for one of us… perhaps both but certainly one." He looked at the ceiling. "Thought I should tell you – we owe you that at least." He brought his gaze back to her. "Vive la France," he said, opened the front door and walked out. "Vive la France," she echoed.

The pilot looked startled as she entered the room. Just her and him. All the way to the coast.

"We must go," she said and explained to him the 20-paces rule. This time she would be leading the way.

Chapter 16

The Café de Biarritz was on the Boulevard Saint-Michel not far from the Gare Montparnasse, the station which in peacetime whisked happy holidaymakers away by the trainload to the Atlantic coast.

Vette waited outside the café for the pilot to catch up. "Say nothing," she said and pushed open the door.

It was warm inside. A man sitting at a table on his own looked up, prodded by the waft of cold air that accompanied their entrance. Vette avoided his glance. She nodded at the patron behind the counter. He was wiping its top with a large white cloth.

Most of the tables were taken, surrounded by groups of students, too busy arguing and chattering to pay any attention to the schoolgirl and young man pushing past.

Vette found a free table at the back of the café, next to the door to the toilets – always leave a way out Nina had told her when they were singing for the German soldiers. Besides it was warmer away from the front door, hidden in the fug of the café.

A student from the largest table stood up, laughing as he did so. He was dressed as a Zazou in a baggy dark suit, dark glasses pushed back on to his forehead. She could see the umbrella hooked over his chair. Vette leaned forward, anxious to get a good look at him. He might be a friend of Paulie's, she might know him…

The Zazou swaggered to the counter and leaned over it. He swept the café with a glance, caught Vette looking at him and grinned. She lowered her gaze. What was she thinking? She needed to be see-through… what if he came over and tried to talk to the pilot? It would take him less than a minute to work out the pilot was not French. What if he was an informer?

"Stupid," hissed Vette. The pilot looked at her. The waiter appeared. "Oui?" His sudden appearance made Vette jump. He had a face that looked as if it had been squashed, his nose spread almost flat, a boxer's face.

"Um, are the eggs from your own chickens or are they from the countryside?" She said it just as Raymond instructed, apart from the 'um.'

"All our eggs are laid in the countryside and arrive fresh every day." The waiter didn't even look up as he gave the required reply. This was Jo le Boxeur. "So what can I get you?"

Vette realised she was starving. "Two plates of the day, please."

It was macaroni with mashed swede and the faintest sprinkle of cheese on top. "Extra cheese for you," said the waiter with a wink as he put the plates down.

Vette wolfed hers down. It didn't taste of much but was warm and felt good in her belly. The pilot pushed his around the plate in between small mouthfuls. He put down his fork – he was still too used to Royal Air Force rations back in Britain, hadn't been in France long enough to become desperate.

"Non?" said Vette.

"Non," echoed the pilot. So Vette took his plate and scraped it clean. Washing-up didn't take much doing in Paris.

The waiter brought them a couple of chestnut coffees. The pilot took a sip and grimaced. Vette scowled at him, took a sip herself and tried her best not to copy his pained face. They sat in silence, waiting for instructions. Jo le Boxeur, cleared their plates then paid them no attention.

The warmth and the hubbub of the café washed over Vette. She felt her eyelids growing heavy. If only she could shut them, just for a little while.

"Huh," she said and sat bolt upright. The pilot was staring at her, his face even whiter than usual. She must have dozed off. A hand tapped her shoulder. She looked round. A gendarme towered above her.

"Papers please," he said. She looked towards the toilet door. She wouldn't make it, and even if she did the pilot certainly wouldn't. Maybe if she created a scene he could make a dash for it. But where would he go? It was hopeless.

She handed over her papers. The gendarme studied them, reached into his pocket and added another document to them, closed hers and handed them back.

"Merci," he said. He had another set of papers in his hand – she hadn't seen where it had come from – and passed it towards the pilot.

"And these must be yours, Monsieur... you dropped them I think, they were on the floor. You must be more careful."

The pilot took them, staring blankly at the policeman, who tapped the peak of his cap, nodded at them both – a nod to end their secret exchange – and moved on to the next table.

"Papers please," he said. Three students dug into their pockets and Vette noticed the silence that settled over the café with the gendarmes' arrival – there was another checking papers on the far side. She took a deep breath, and she'd fallen asleep. What if…

That was not the way. There were always 'what ifs.' It wouldn't happen again. She opened her papers and unfolded the document inside – a travel permit from Paris to the Brittany coast – and tickets for the night train. The permit was in the name of Valérie Saunier. That might work, it was close enough to the name on her papers – a bored guard surely wouldn't study a schoolgirl's papers closely.

She put her hand out and the pilot passed over his papers. His papers and travel permit matched, Joseph Franc, a salesman. She laid them on the table and pointed at the name and the occupation. She leaned towards him and whispered: "Learn this."

They sat another hour until darkness settled over the streets. Vette led the pilot out, nodding a farewell at Jo le Boxeur, who grunted a reply. Outside she linked arms with the pilot.

"Now we must walk – it is best not to go on to the train until the last minute. I will call you Joseph. If I speak to you on the train, nod at me as if you understand and sometimes say 'Oui' – say it like 'we' okay? You can also say 'oui, oui' – 'wee-wee'…"

She grinned at him and was relieved to see a small smile offered in return. She had to make him more relaxed. At the moment he looked so scared the Gestapo would spot him in their sleep.

"You can sleep on the train – I will keep a look out. Now we've time to kill so I'm going to give you a French lesson – like you are back at school again… can you remember school or are you too old?"

She offered another smile so he would know she was being silly.

"Still young at heart," he said, his smile a little bigger this time. "School was damn good fun – I'd rather be at school than stuck here…"

"Well, thank you very much – didn't think I was that bad." Vette nudged the pilot and he let out a little laugh, as though he couldn't help it.

"Phew," thought Vette and began the lesson.

Chapter 17

Vette pinched her cheeks and rubbed her eyes. She glanced up at the clock. Their timing was perfect. Now they needed fortune to smile on them.

She watched the pilot approach the barrier. There was a French ticket inspector and two German soldiers. This would be their last check of a long, dull day. Perfect, thought Vette and began to run. It was four minutes until the train was due to depart.

By the time she reached the barrier, jostling up against the pilot, waving her papers and tickets in the air, tears were marking her cheeks.

"Please, please," she sobbed. The pilot turned around, his papers clutched in his hand. "My mother… she's already on the train. I cannot miss it, I cannot…"

She tripped and crashed into the pilot, who joined her

in tumbling to the ground. One of the guards guffawed. The ticket inspector tutted. The other guard helped Vette to her feet.

"Thank you," she said and sniffed loudly. "Here, my papers, my permit." She fussed over her papers, trying to get them in the right order.

The train let out an impatient hoot.

"Ohhhhh," squealed Vette.

"Go, go," said one guard. "Both of you, run or you'll miss it."

"Wait," said the other. "We haven't…"

"No, no, she's just a child," said the first guard. "Go – go, quick." Vette didn't need to be asked twice. She ran, and the pilot ran with her.

The train let out a squeal of its own, the carriages protesting at the engine's insistence it was time to go. The wheels began their first slow turn as Vette reached the iron step to the last carriage. She leapt up it, turned and put a hand out to help the pilot. He took it and scrambled on. Vette waved at the guards, the one who'd wanted to check their papers was hooting with laughter at their frantic dash.

"Keep laughing, just you keep laughing," muttered Vette as the train gathered speed and headed off into the night.

"Bonne," said the pilot, who seemed to have come alive now they were away from the apartment and on the run.

"Oui," said Vette. "Très bonne. Now let's find a seat."

"Wee-wee," said the pilot and giggled like a schoolboy.

She opened the door to the inside of the carriage. "Shhh now," she cautioned. "The Gestapo are everywhere."

The smile dropped from the pilot's face at the mention of the G-word. It had that effect.

As she stepped into the carriage Vette caught sight of a man ducking through the door at the far end. For a moment she thought she recognised him. But it couldn't have been… she was tired and on edge. She walked down the carriage looking in each compartment. They were all busy. She needed to be careful where they sat. She needed to be careful in everything they did. She would get this one home, make up for… she shook her head, mumbling a "non". What had Raymond said? Don't look back.

They went on into the next carriage. The first compartment had the curtains drawn. Vette didn't like not being able to see in.

It was another two carriages before she found a suitable compartment, occupied only by an elderly couple and a young girl. The girl woke when Vette slid the door open. She apologised for their arrival, the pilot smiled and nodded. The window seats were free so they took them.

A swish of movement in the corridor caught Vette's eye. Once more she saw the flap of a coat as a man passed. There was something familiar about that coat. She shook her head once more; get on with it.

She smiled at the old couple. The girl had curled up again and seemed already asleep.

"Pardon," Vette whispered. "Sorry for waking your granddaughter."

"That's quite all right, my dear," said the old woman, her voice carrying the sound of the waves. In the dull light of the night-time compartment, her weather-beaten face looked lined by life.

"You're going home to the sea?"

The woman cackled. "You think I'm a mermaid? Yes, my dear, we're going home. We collected our granddaughter – Paris is no place for a child at this time."

The train was still gathering speed, rocking gently. The city, its lights blacked out by war, slipped by in the darkness. The old woman studied Vette, then swung her gaze to the pilot.

"Your brother is a tired man."

The pilot had sat down and shut his eyes. Vette had told

him it was best to pretend to sleep all the way to avoid being drawn into conversation.

Vette nodded. "Yes. Do you know Saint-Brieuc?"

"That's where you are going?"

"Yes."

The old woman sucked her teeth. "Always lots of Boche on the platform there – have been for a couple of weeks now, as if they know something about the people who get off the Paris train in Saint-Brieuc." She leaned forward, towards Vette and Vette could have sworn she smelt the sea. "Best to get off the station before, Lamballe... saves time you know, no queues, no-one to check your papers, my dear, not usually."

"But we have to..."

"You can walk to Saint-Brieuc from Lamballe – at that time of the day there's always a farmer or delivery boy heading that way, they'll give you a lift. But up to you my dear, up to you."

She sighed. "Now you sleep, like your brother. I'll wake you in plenty of time."

Trust no-one, trust no-one – the creed of the Resistance had been hammered home to Vette day after day in the museum. But there was something about this old woman, she was like everybody's Granny wrapped up in one.

Trust no-one, trust no-one, whispered in Vette's head, over and over like a stuck gramophone record. She was exhausted. Now they had made the train she could feel tiredness trying to tuck her in for the night.

Trust no-one, trust no-one. You had to trust someone... didn't you? Vette slept.

Chapter 18

Vette jerked awake with a gasp. She glanced round the carriage. The others were asleep. She checked her watch. They were four hours out of Paris. The door to the compartment was open a finger's width. Had a noise woken her? The door opening?

Maybe the old woman had opened it earlier to let some air into the compartment. Maybe the ticket inspector had poked his head in and decided to let them sleep. No – ticket inspectors weren't like that. He would have had them all up.

She tugged the door wide enough to slip into the corridor and closed it tight behind her. The lights were off. She looked right and could make nothing out in the dark. She went left. A sudden light at the end of the corridor brought her to a halt, the flare of a match lighting a cigarette and revealing a face beneath the brim of a hat.

"Raymond?"

Vette walked on towards the glow of the cigarette.

"Raymond is that you?"

The man said nothing. Vette hesitated. The initial lift in her spirits when she recognised him came to a grinding halt. What was he doing here? Why was he lurking in the corridor?

She was in front of him now. His arm shot out and pulled her towards him. He pushed her against the outside door to the carriage.

"Raymond!"

"Shhhh," he said. He flicked the cigarette out the door's open window. The wind whipped at Vette's hair. He clamped a hand over her mouth.

"Listen to me," he hissed. "You're in great, great danger – you must do exactly as I say and we'll both live. Understand?"

Vette stared at him wide-eyed. He stared back, on edge, just as wide-eyed. His breath smelt. Of cigarettes, and something else. Did fear have a smell?

"Understand?"

She nodded. "Not a word," he added. She nodded. He took his hand away.

"When you get off at Saint-Brieuc, you'll be let through the German checks – meet your contact and do as he instructs. You'll be followed to the hiding place and then followed to the rendezvous with the English boat where we'll catch them all. The rendezvous, it's somewhere up the coast, I don't know where – I have to deliver them the whole route. I told them I only know Paris but they said the whole escape route, they want it all. You help me and I'll see to it you're okay. They won't shoot you."

"I don't understand…"

"Do as I say and I'll save you."

"Wait, no… it's… it's you… you are… it's not Alain is it – you said it was Alain…"

"What're you talking about?" He glanced down the corridor. "Get back in your compartment, quick… in case the Englishman wakes up – you must not make him suspicious. He mustn't know he's walking into a trap."

"You said it was Alain… but it's not is it? It's you, you… the pilots in the park, your telephone call – it was to the Gestapo, it was wasn't it? Raymond, you're the traitor… you're a traitor…"

Raymond pushed his arm against her throat, pressing her back against the door and cutting off her words. Her hands scrabbled against the door and her left one found the handle.

"If you want to live, you must do as I say." He pressed

harder, leaning against Vette. The wind howled in her ears.

"Okay?"

"Cécile," she said. She wanted to shout. "Where's Cécile?"

"Never mind, Cécile, they'll have her soon enough, she won't get away, she won't be able to tell anyone what we've done."

Vette slid her right arm through the window. Her head was nearly leaning out of it.

"You are a traitor," she said to Raymond and pushed hard down on the door handle.

Pressed against Vette, Raymond had no time to find his balance as the door swung open. Vette gasped as she swung with it, she tried to split her bodyweight between her right arm on the window ledge and her left hand on the door handle, hanging on for dear life.

There was nothing for Raymond to hang on to. Vette saw a look of surprise widen his eyes as he wobbled for a moment on the edge, knowing he was going to fall no matter what he did. The wind whipped off his hat and he fell.

He may have made a sound but the whistle of the wind around the carriages and the drumming of the train's wheels stopped it reaching Vette's ears. One moment he was there, the next he wasn't.

Trust no-one, trust no-one. Vette closed her eyes. For a moment she thought about letting go. A hand grabbed one of her legs.

"Hang on!" A voice in English. Yes, Grandpere, I will hang on. She opened her eyes. The pilot was reaching for her. He bundled her back into the carriage and then pulled the door shut. They sat on the floor in the dark, the train chuntering on, *must-get-to-the-coast-must-get-to-the-coast-must-get-to-the-coast…*

No-one came, no-one had seen or heard a thing.

Vette wagged her finger at the pilot. "No English," she said. "No English." The pilot nodded. She stood up, her arms ached. The pilot stood too. "Merci," she said.

"Wee-wee," said the pilot, grinned, patted her on the back and headed back to the compartment.

Neither of them slept for the rest of the night. The wheels struck up a new tune in Vette's mind. *Raymond-the-traitor, Raymond-the-traitor, Raymond-the-traitor*. They stopped at a station and afterwards the tune changed once more as the train strained to pick up pace again. *Cécile, Cécile, Cécile, Cécile*. Vette closed her eyes and kept the tears trapped inside.

Dawn arrived and soon after they pulled into a small station.

"Here," said the old woman. "You get off here."

They dropped down on to the platform and watched the train chug off. Two other men got off, old men, probably farmers who'd gone up to Paris to sell butter on the black market. Vette let them leave, undoing and retying her laces several times. Outside the station they found themselves on a cobbled street, a long row of cottages on either side. The road ran straight from east, where the autumn sun was doing all it could be bothered to warm the day, to west. They could see the road running out of the village.

"Saint-Brieuc, 12 km" announced a sign pointing west. How long would it would take to walk 12 kilometres? How long would the contact wait outside the station in Saint-Brieuc? Waiting was dangerous, especially with the Germans on the lookout. She didn't really have any idea how far 12 kilometres was. They didn't have long – their time was running out. She thought of the metre measuring sticks at school. If she laid them end-to-end how many would make up…

"Look," said the pilot. A truck was making its way down the street. As it got closer they saw the driver, on his own in the cab, was in uniform, the grey of the German army. The pilot stepped back towards the station. Vette stepped forward and raised her hand into a thumbs-up.

"Jerry," hissed the pilot. "Hunnnnn…"

"Just smile and nod, pretend you cannot speak," said Vette.

The lorry slowed. She glanced at the pilot and saw the look of alarm in his eyes. "Trust me," she said, and then again. "You can trust me."

The lorry stopped a little distance from them. The driver eyed them through the dusty windscreen. Vette flashed a smile at him and approached the passenger side.

"Do you speak French?" she said.

The driver shook his head. "A little, little," he said.

"Um, help us," she said. "My brother and me, no money, need to get home to Saint-Brieuc, please… please." The tone of her voice and the accompanying gestures – as if she was playing charades – worked as much as what she said. She pointed west.

The driver was old for a soldier. Perhaps he looked down and saw his own children, in trouble, relying on the kindness of strangers. He was a supply driver, taking food and clothing from one base to another; he didn't want to be in France, he wanted to be at home, with his wife and his children, his dear children. He gestured for them to get in. He was bored of the barrack room. He wanted not to be a soldier, just for half an hour.

He chatted happily as they drove the road to Saint-

Brieuc. He spoke in German and Vette did not understand a word but offered him a smile, a nod and the odd comment: "really," "good," "interesting," and "aww, bless" when his tone of voice suggested so. The driver beamed back.

"Here," said Vette just after they passed the sign for Saint-Brieuc. They clambered down outside a row of small houses and waved a cheery farewell to their driver, who gave an equally cheery response. A curtain twitched behind them.

"Come on," said Vette. "Let's find the station."

Chapter 19

The station filled one side of the town's main square. They stood on the opposite side, in the shadow of a large church. Two solid towers guarded its heavy red door.

The train had come and gone; so, it seemed, had their contact. Two men were standing outside the station. They were not in uniform but might as well have carried a sign. Both wore long leather coats and wide-brimmed hats pulled low in an attempt to hide busy eyes.

It was market day and between Vette and the Gestapo men the square was busy with farmers unloading their wagons, their wives setting up stall. The men led their horses, big and sturdy, clopping to the stone trough in the square and gossiped as the animals drank.

There was a café on the left-hand side of the square, its

owner, wearing a pristine white apron, carefully putting out his tables and chairs, expecting a busy day.

Mustn't linger, thought Vette, mustn't attract attention. The locals would spot strangers, and if just one of them was an informer…

The farmers, unloading done, horses watered, were filling the tables outside the café, ignoring the pained glances of their wives, who continued to prepare the stalls. The owner was joined by a young woman in a blue smock and a waitress's apron, her dark hair curling past her shoulders. She laughed and joked with the farmers as they ordered breakfast.

The distance from the church to the café seemed enormous; every step of the way they would be under the searching eyes of the men in leather coats. She turned and led the pilot into the archway covering the church door. She tried the handle; it turned.

She'd never been in a church before. She shivered. It was cooler inside and still, the hustle and bustle of the market kept out by the thick walls. She pointed to a pew and slipped in after the pilot. She needed to collect her thoughts.

"Bonjour."

Vette jumped, the pilot leapt to his feet. The priest had come from nowhere.

"Heard the door," he said, walking down the aisle that

separated the rows of pews. He stopped at the end of theirs, cutting off their escape. "Not from the town are you."

It wasn't a question. "Come off the train? I didn't see you at the station." He sat down on the pew and slid along its surface, smoothed and shone by Sunday-best dresses and trousers for the last hundred years.

"Father Renoir," he said offering his hand.

Vette shook it. "Vette," she said, "and my brother."

"Does he have a name, your brother?" Father Renoir leaned across Vette and pushed his hand towards the pilot.

"Um, Joseph," mumbled Vette.

"Can you not say for yourself, my son?" said Father Renoir as the pilot took his hand and grunted.

"I'm sorry?" said Father Renoir.

"He cannot speak Father."

"No?" The priest frowned, lent back and looked up towards the distant ceiling of his church. "We have seen several like your poor brother in recent months. Perhaps it is hoped a trip to the sea will bring back his speech? A miracle cure by the ocean?"

"Um," said Vette. The other end of the pew was blocked off by the wall.

The priest stood up. "That's a fine school you go to. I know it well – you are far from home. Your uniform, well…"

He smiled down at her. "Seen better times, hasn't it?" He stepped into the aisle.

"If you want to help your brother I suggest you take the road to Plouha. The walk will take you four hours, perhaps longer. There find the café, ask for Monsieur Le Cornec, tell him Father Renoir sent you. He will say to you 'How is Father Renoir?' You reply 'Father Renoir has the first signs of an autumn cold.' Understand? Exactly those words."

Vette nodded. "Come," said the priest, "I'll let you out the back way."

He fetched a large key and as it clunked in the lock added one final piece of advice. "Listen out for engines – only the Germans drive here, and they are not so keen on young men heading for the coast to find a cure."

It was good advice. Twice they had to dive into the ditch on the long plod to Plouha. The first time an old truck groaned past, the second a motorcycle with a sidecar screeched by.

Vette's uniform looked even less like that of one of Paris' smartest schools by the time they trudged into the village. It was late afternoon, the clouds gathering as the day lengthened. Her feet ached and her head throbbed. The café was quiet and became quieter still when they entered.

"Monsieur Le Cornec?"

The man behind the counter gave a small nod, lips pursed, eyes assessing her.

"Father Renoir sent us."

"How is Father Renoir?"

"Father Renoir has the first signs of an autumn cold."

Monsieur Le Cornec nodded as if assessing what she had said and pointed to a table.

"Have a seat." His voice was soft and careful.

They sat, grateful of the chance to rest, and were given parsnip soup and a little bread, wolfing it down as the evening began to drain light from the day. As Vette was wiping the last trace from her bowl with her final corner of bread, the bell above the door tinkled and a girl came in. She smiled at Monsieur Le Cornec and stopped by their table.

"Come," she said. "Ten paces," she added and the bell tinkled as she left. They followed her down the main street. It turned right and headed downhill. They could smell the sea.

The girl stopped at a cottage on the edge of the village. She waited for them to catch up before knocking. Three sharp raps on the door and one longer one. The door opened and she tilted her head. She didn't follow them in.

A young man, about Paulie's age, possibly a little older, dressed in flannel trousers and a shirt with sleeves rolled up over thick arms, stood by the door. His arms, like his face were tanned, the look of someone who spends a great deal of his time outside. He smiled at them.

"Please, make yourselves comfortable…" He waved a hand around the single room that made up the downstairs of the cottage. A couple of easy chairs were arranged to flank the fireplace. There was a wooden dining table in the middle of the room and at the far end what passed for a kitchen. In one corner a curved metal staircase led upstairs.

"We've a long night ahead before the boat comes. I'll make coffee."

The pilot headed straight for one of the easy chairs and collapsed into it with a happy groan. He hummed a tune to himself, beginning to believe he was actually going to make it home after all.

The man made for the kitchen.

"I must talk to you," said Vette.

He lit the stove and pulled a kettle on to the hob; his back to her.

"What about?" He turned to face her.

The kettle whistled. The Resistance fighter turned back to it.

"We've been betrayed," she said to his back.

He took the kettle from the hob and poured boiling water into three cups. "Go on," he said.

"The whole network, Raymond's network – it's exposed. It's him, Raymond… Raymond is a traitor."

She told him everything she knew. He listened in silence. "Wait here," he said when she was finished. He climbed the stairs and returned a few minutes later with a radio. "You must listen – the French time is starting soon. Listen for our code – if they say 'Tout bien à la Maison d'Alphonse' a British boat will be here tonight."

He crossed to the door, took a coat hanging from a nearby hook. "I must tell others what you told me. If I don't come back… leave at midnight, follow the road to the lighthouse, there's a track that runs to the left, take it, follow the cliffs to the third bay, you'll find a cottage, the house of Uncle Alphonse. Knock like this…" he repeated the knock the girl had used earlier… "…tell him Captain Camille sent you and he will take you to the creek where the ship will be. Got that?"

Amélie nodded.

"Good," he said. "Be careful on the cliffs in the dark, the path… it can be difficult to follow."

The pilot looked up, then stood, sensing he'd missed something important. He came over to Vette.

"What is it?"

"I…" began Vette.

Camille pulled on his coat. He switched to English for the pilot's benefit. "There is a traitor. It's the end for her…"

"The end!"

"For me!"

Vette and the pilot spoke at once.

"You can't work for us anymore," said Camille. "We'll try and hide you, somewhere down south but you can't go back to Paris… perhaps in a few months but not for the moment. We can't have you here either, too dangerous."

"She can come to England."

Vette and Camille turned to the pilot. "Yes, after what she's done – taking her to England, it's the least I can do."

Camille shrugged. "Up to you," he said, reverting back to French. "I just need rid of you as soon as possible. You're a danger to all of us."

He nodded at her. "Good luck… and thank you – you've given us a chance." He opened the door and closed it quickly behind him. Vette stared at the door.

"I'm Tony," said the pilot suddenly. He put his hand out. "I want you to know my name. Because... because without you I would... well, I wouldn't be here for starters."

"Amélie," she replied. "Amélie Dreyfus. That is my name. My real name."

Chapter 20

Uncle Alphonse wore the heavy orange trousers of a fisherman and spoke only in grunts. For the two hours they were with him he did not utter a single word. There was an hour of walking, down to a beach then round a bay, the soft sound of the waves washing over the sand, then a climb and a final careful clamber along a path cut into the cliff edge before they turned a corner and dropped down into a narrow creek that interrupted the cliffs.

Once they found the old stone jetty, long ago a smuggler's haunt, there was another hour of waiting, Amélie shivering as the cold crept up her legs no matter how much she stomped her feet.

At last Uncle Alphonse gave a happier grunt and flashed a torch out to sea, once, twice, three times. Moments later the purr of a powerful engine rolled out of the dark and a British torpedo boat bumped softly against the jetty.

"Merci," said Amélie, shaking Uncle Alphonse's hand. He grunted and gave the slightest of nods. Hands reached down from the boat and pulled Tony up.

"And her," said Tony.

The hands reached down for Amélie. She stood on deck and raised a hand as Uncle Alphonse was swallowed by the night. "Au revoir," she said.

She wasn't saying goodbye to Uncle Alphonse, not even to France. She was saying goodbye to Vette. Because Vette was finished. She let out a heavy sigh and followed Tony below decks. What, she wondered, lay ahead for Amélie Dreyfus?

* * *

"School I should think," said Tony and drained his glass. He was drinking brandy. "Just the one to warm me," he said.

Amélie shook her head when the torpedo boat's captain offered her one. "Just a schoolgirl," said Tony. "Not old enough for a brandy but old enough to save my life – this is one clever young lady and a damned brave one too. Braver than any of us, you know – I couldn't do what her and her chaps do, would drive a man crazy. No, thank you, I'll stick to my aeroplane."

Amélie blushed. She didn't like people talking about her like that. She never thought of herself as brave. She just wanted to get her Maman back, and Paulie and Papa, and the only way to do that was for the Germans to be beaten.

"Yes, school – one of England's best I should have thought and we have the best bloody schools in the world, Miss Dreyfus, so you are in for a treat."

Tony seemed intent on making up for not having been allowed to talk for so long.

"No doubt they'll fix you up in some boarding school because… because, well, it's just you on your own isn't it. No home to go back to each night. Can't be helped and you'll soon settle in – nothing like an English boarding school for a proper education, reading, writing and that other thing – ha! Made me the man I am today I suppose."

It was just the two of them now, the captain and the crew back on deck as the torpedo boat skimmed across the waves, course set for Plymouth on England's south-west coast.

Amélie shook her head.

"Can't believe your luck, eh? You deserve it, Miss Dreyfus, absolutely deserve it. For you the war is over… lucky thing, eh?"

"Over… no, but I…"

"Yes, you've done your bit now leave the rest to us chaps to finish off."

Amélie opened and shut her mouth. School? Non, non, non. NON. And what was boarding school? School on a boat that you had to board? Like a school ship? That sounded interesting… but non. There was no time for school, not when Maman, Papa and Paulie were in German hands.

The idea of lessons and homework filled her with dread. She'd made a vow to Maman. She must get back to France, she must fight, and she wouldn't stop until Paulie and her parents were home again, all of them together in the apartment. Playing hide and seek.

They arrived in Plymouth with dawn. She felt sick as the boat motored slowly through the harbour, whether it was from the sea or the thought of what lay ahead she didn't know, and didn't care. She had to find a way back across the English Channel.

There were two cars waiting on the jetty, standing beside them two men, both wearing long coats – faded brown raincoats not leather ones – and hats with peaks angled over the left eye as if they thought it gave them an air of mystery. They watched as the boat bumped against the jetty and two sailors jumped ashore holding ropes they wound into place.

One of the raincoat men was staring at Amélie as she walked up the gangplank behind Tony. She stared back, lifting her chin in defiance.

"Well…" Tony had made it back on to English soil. "This is so long then – I should say thank you, Miss Dreyfus… what you've done for me, well, you saved my…"

Amélie lifted a hand. "Non, non…" She shrugged. "It's done." The pilot's attempt at a fond farewell was not what she wanted. Not when she was trying to stop the despair rising within her.

"Tell you what, old girl, I'll find out what school they pop you in then I'll dash down at weekends in the motor and whisk you up to London for a slap-up luncheon." Amélie smiled, weakly. She had no idea what he was talking about. He leaned closer to her. "They may be damn fine schools but I have to admit the grub's a bloody disaster. Always has been, always will be – bread and butter pudding, eucccchhh." He stepped back, patted his stomach. "Quite comforting actually, things staying the same, especially at a time like this."

He shook her hand.

"Thank you, Miss Dreyfus."

"Are we done here?"

The man who'd been staring at Amélie was in front of

them. He was tall and square jawed. But it was his eyes that caught her attention. They were a steely grey and when he looked at her Amélie felt as if he could see inside.

"That's your car, Flight Lieutenant," he said, gesturing with a dismissive flick of his right hand. "Off you trot, there's a war to win you know."

"Right-o, sir," said Tony, standing up straight and flinging his right hand into a salute.

He winked at Amélie, threw a wave in the direction of the boat and its crew and made for the other car. Its driver already had the back door open.

"Shall we," said the grey-eyed man. It wasn't a question. He gestured at his car. A driver leapt out and opened the back door.

"Good, good," said the man once they were settled on the back seat and to Amélie's surprise a smile axed its way across his face.

"Welcome to England, Miss Dreyfus. I am Captain Selwyn Jepson. We received a message from Captain Camille explaining the situation and..."

"What's going to happen to me?"

"I see," said Jepson and Amélie caught a flicker of irritation at her interruption. "You're an impatient sort." He said it as if he was taking notes.

"No, Captain," said Amélie, interrupting again. "I am the sort who knows there's a war on and there's no time to waste."

"Ah, touché, Miss Dreyfus, touché," said Jepson.

"So?"

"Well, yes, let's see… we have a school for you, Symington Hall. Just need to tie up a few loose ends first… can't abide loose ends – one tug and everything unravels."

He lent forward and touched the driver on the shoulder. The car started with a growl. "We'll begin, shall we Miss Dreyfus." Again it wasn't a question. He took a notebook from his coat pocket, followed by a pen and tapped the pen on the notebook's hard cover. "So, easy one to start with – how old are you?"

"Seventeen." The lie tripped off her tongue before she even knew it was gone.

Jepson cocked his head to one side. "Seventeen… we thought you were younger."

"I need to go back to France," said Amélie. "I want to go back, I must go back – to the Resistance. I need to find Cécile, I need to find…" She shrugged. "I have to go back." If they knew how old she really was there was no way she would get back across the Channel – it would be all aboard school and terrible food for goodness knows how long.

152

"All in good time," said Jepson. "Questions first."

"No… first I have one for you."

Jepson raised an eyebrow but said nothing.

"How do you know my name?"

"Ah, Miss Dreyfus…" He sighed. "I do hope you are not going to be tricky. I'll be honest with you as I'm sure you'll be with me."

Amélie glanced at him out of the corner of her eye. She knew how it worked; he would be as honest with her as he needed to be and no more. Just as she would be with him. She could play his game too.

"We know you are from Paris, we know your name and we know you are an orphan. We know you worked for the Musée de l'Homme network…"

He knew a lot – the network must have been in touch with London – but he didn't know about Maman, Papa and Paulie, and Amélie decided she would not tell him.

"We need to know what happened to the network, why you've ended up here… in this game, Miss Dreyfus, one can't be too careful. For all I know you might be the traitor and then where will we be."

Another of his non-question questions, and from the glance shot her way Amélie could take a good guess where she would be. Somewhere pretty unpleasant.

"Let's not go there shall we, Miss Dreyfus. Answer my questions and we'll have you at Symington in time for supper."

The questions, real questions, began, and she answered them all. She told him about Cécile and Alain, about Raymond, about what he'd said to her, about the safe house discovered by the Gestapo, how she'd told Captain Camille about the betrayal.

"And where is Raymond, do you think?"

She told Jepson of their confrontation on the train. He raised another eyebrow as she described opening the train door and Raymond plunging into the darkness. Then he shut his notebook and screwed the lid back on to his pen.

"Cécile..." said Amélie. "Is Cécile safe? I have to know."

Jepson slipped the pen inside his jacket.

"I said I'd be honest with you..." Jepson paused, as if gathering his thoughts. "This is... how best to put it... a job... a job most people will not get out of in one piece. I think you know that, you're a bright girl. As for your Cécile... well, let's just say I don't think she will be in one piece for much longer."

"But you can't be certain?"

"There is little I can be certain of."

"I must go back – I'm old enough, I can do it. I can find her. You need me. Send me back – you must."

"Must we," said Jepson. He looked out the window. They were out in the country, brown fields and threadbare autumn hedgerows whizzed past. He spoke to the window.

"You may be bright, Miss Dreyfus, and have certain talents we admire but you're also young, too young. This is not child's play. Finish your schooling and then perhaps – perhaps, we shall talk. Understand?"

Amélie opened her mouth, ready to let her anger out but closed it just in time. She nodded, mouth shut tight. Jepson turned to look at her, those eyes boring into her. He nodded back. He seemed pleased with her response.

"Ah," he said as the driver turned off the road and stopped in front of a large pair of metal gates topped with a row of spikes. "We're here."

Chapter 21

"Pour-ridge?"

"Oui, porridge, that is how they say it."

"But what is it?"

Amélie lifted her spoon and let the brown sludge slop back into the bowl. This was her sixth or seventh or eighth or ninth morning at Symington Hall, she wasn't sure because they were all the same. It was the first time anyone had spoken directly to her, not counting teachers or teasing. Like Amélie, Hélène didn't belong here and when you didn't belong at Symington Hall you stuck out like a glowing-red sore thumb.

"Ribbit… ribbit… ribbit…"

Amélie looked round. At the end of the table sat Margaret Brown, the head girl of Dickens, the boarding house Amélie had been placed in. Margaret didn't like Amélie, nor did she care for Hélène. Amélie had no idea why because she'd spoken exactly one word to Margaret Brown.

"Hello," she said when the headmistresses, Miss Dit and Miss Dot, showed Amélie to her dormitory. Margaret Brown had been instructing a group of younger girls how to make their beds properly; hospital corners, wrinkle-less blankets and flat pillows or 100 lines. Then she'd turned on Amélie.

"Look at the froggies ribbitting away to each other, ribbit, froggy, ribbit, froggy."

"Ignore her," said Hélène. "It's the best way, I promise you."

Amélie stared at Margaret's tea cup. It was turned upside down. Margaret insisted it was placed like that when the juniors laid the table the evening before. 'It only takes a speck of dust to ruin my breakfast tea because I have very sensitive taste buds,' she declared.

Without fail she turned her cup over when she finished her pour-ridge; Margaret was a girl who liked everything just so. Which was why she screamed when she turned it over and a small, brown frog leapt out.

And what Margaret did everyone in Dickens followed. One by one the screaming spread down the table and it didn't just stop at Dickens, but crossed over to Shakespeare – the houses were named after great English writers – and then Ambler. Soon the entire dining room was in uproar. Amid the hubbub Amélie took Hélène's hand and they slipped out the side door (the one supposed to be for teachers and prefects only).

Back in the dormitory, Hélène gave Amélie a knowing look.

"Quoi?" said Amélie, relieved to be speaking French again. "I ignored her, as you said." She grinned at Hélène, took her hands and they sat down on Amélie's bed. "That was kind of you to move places to sit next to me. It's so good to have someone to talk to. How long have you been here? Where are you from? How do we get out of here?"

"We don't – you must have seen the guards at the gate. They patrol the wall at night as well."

"To stop us escaping? From school?"

"Well, no – they're guarding us. There are important children here, or rather their parents are important – ministers in the government and such like. They worry Nazi spies will try and kidnap us."

"Us?"

"My father – he is, well was, in the Belgian government.

What's yours? He must be something important for you to be here, at the best school in England."

"Papa? Um, he's… well, never mind… TONY – that's it…"

Amélie's sudden shout made Hélène start. "Sorry – but that's it. I'll write to Tony and he'll come and take me to London for the weekend and then I can, well, I'll think of something."

"Who is Tony? You cannot write to him – they check the letters, Miss Tick and Tock, read every one and cross out in thick black ink anything they don't like."

The bell interrupted them, clanging insistently from its tower. The bell ran their day; told them when to get up – a quarter to seven – when to go to sleep – 8 o'clock sharp, and no talking after lights out – and everything in between, lunch, tea, break, games time…

Lesson time. Amélie sighed. She had double Latin. 'What is the point of Latin?' she asked Miss Amat, the teacher, who in return gave her 100 lines. Latin was followed by a run around the large school grounds being shouted at by Miss Shipton. Then more lessons that made no sense to her, then something soggy and brown for tea, then homework then bed beneath a thin blanket in this cold dorm. If this was one of the best schools in England, Amélie could not imagine the worst.

"If it comes to it I'll swim the Channel," she stated as they hurried down the tower staircase towards Miss Amat's classroom. The morning swim, 10 lengths before breakfast in an outdoor pool (being shouted at by Miss Shipton), was the only part of the day Amélie looked forward to. She loved diving into the water, the sharp shock of the cold waking every bit of her, the ease with which she moved through the water, arms and legs kicking together, the glow of satisfaction afterwards as she headed for the dining hall. And then it disappeared in the slopping of the pour-ridge into her bowl as the gloom of the long, dull day ahead settled itself around her.

How long had it been? She promised herself she'd add up her chalk marks at bedtime – she'd swiped a piece of chalk on the way out of Miss Amat's classroom. Each night she made a mark behind her bedhead. She'd seen it in a film, a flic in Paris. A man wrongly sent to prison by a corrupt policeman chalked up each day of his wrongful punishment. That's what it felt like – she'd been locked up for something she hadn't done.

The hero escaped in the end, made a rope with bed sheets from the prison hospital and disappeared into the night. The film ended happily with the corrupt policeman in jail and the man handing the policeman a piece of chalk through the cell bars before turning up his collar and heading off down the street whistling.

Amélie suspected in real life, especially in times of war, happy endings were harder to come by. That didn't mean she was going to sit and rot in the damp English countryside for the rest of the year.

The need for patience, Amélie knew fine well, was an important part of being in the Resistance (and Amélie insisted to herself she was a still in the Resistance). As was not doing anything rash (like trying to scale the front gate when the guard went for his tea break – she was halfway up when she came to her senses and slid back down). So she took a deep breath and wrote to Tony.

It took a while for him to reply – after all there was a war on – and Amélie gritted her teeth through more grey days of grey lessons and brown dinners and brown knees after slipping and sliding around the woods on their daily run. One day she slipped in a particularly muddy part, at the far end of the school grounds where the high brick wall surrounding the grounds cut through the woods. She leaned against the wall puffing. Her breath slowed and she noticed a small hole in the wall. She put her fist into it. It was just the right size for a girl's foot, and not far above it was another. They seemed to have been carved into the wall. She looked up and there were more. She traced a zigzag pattern of holes and the odd brick jutting ever so slightly out from the wall. They led all the way to the top.

"GIRRRRRRRRLLLLSSSSS – I AM WAITING!"

Miss Shipton's voice trumpeted through the trees. Amélie ran her hands up the wall. She put one foot in the first hole.

"ONE MINUTE, GIRRRRRRLLLLSSS… OR YOU'LL GO ROUND AGAIN."

Amélie stuck her tongue out in Miss Shipton's direction but started running. She didn't want to go round again. In the back of her mind, she stored away the curious pattern climbing the wall in this hidden corner of the grounds. Just as a good Resistance worker should.

Tony's brief reply made up her mind. "Wonderful to hear from you, old girl. Sorry school is so rotten. Why do you want me to send rope? Busy chasing Jerry across the heavens at the mo, will be down when I can. Chin up, old girl, you've done your bit for King and Country – time to leave the rest to us chaps! Your humble servant, Tony."

"Huh," said Amélie.

"A pilot wrote to you – a real life pilot…" said Hélène.

Amélie shrugged. She opened the dorm window and looked down. It was time to throw patience out of the window and for her to follow.

Chapter 22

It wasn't the dorm window in the end, but a bathroom window on the floor below that Amélie used.

She spent a couple more nights prowling the school, ducking into doorways and hiding under tables to avoid being seen, and that was enough to establish the safest way out. There was a soldier on guard at each of the three doors but none round the rear of the building. The ground floor windows were sealed shut but those on the floor above were not. So Amélie persuaded Hélène to lend her sheet, tied it to her own and dangled it out the second floor bathroom window.

This was the teacher's floor but all was still apart from the rumbling snores coming, as you might expect, from Miss Shipton's bedroom. The bathroom window creaked as

Amélie eased it open. She tied the sheet tight and clambered backwards on to the windowsill.

Hélène was peeking through a crack in the door, keeping an eye on the corridor.

"You sure you won't come?" whispered Amélie.

"Non," said Hélène, "I cannot, I…"

"It's okay," said Amélie. "I understand. Au revoir and thank you."

She lowered herself down and began her descent. It was harder than she expected.

"No happy endings," she whispered to herself.

She felt the sheets tighten and enjoyed a moment of relief when they held. She hung there, arms above her head, legs dangling, the white sheet descending into the inky darkness below like a fishing line disappearing into the depths of the ocean. She'd imagined herself shimmying expertly to the ground, landing without a sound on the gravel pathway and vanishing beneath the cover of the woods, next stop France.

"Amélie… are you all right?"

Hélène's face appeared at the window.

"Um, yes," said Amélie. She loosened her grip and allowed herself to slide a little down the sheet. The wall scratched a hole in her woollen tights and the skin from both knees – she was dressed in all she had, the uniform she'd been given when she arrived at the school, a dark blue pinafore over a white blouse and a saggy woollen overcoat on top.

"Owww," she hissed. She looked down. Her feet were at the top of the ground-floor windows.

Hélène made a startled noise. Amélie looked up, Hélène's face was not there. Then it was. She leaned out, trying to cut the distance her words had to travel.

"I think someone's coming," she said then pulled the window shut, jerking the sheets as she did so.

Amélie's right hand lost its grip and she began to slide down the sheet. Her feet knocked on the window – it was a classroom so deserted – and then the palm of her left hand began to burn as the sheet scorched through her fingers. She let go.

It was not far to the ground, but the impact was enough to drive the air from her lungs. She lay on her back, the gravel poking into her from every angle. Her knees smarted, her palm stung, her back hurt. But when the window opened and a face appeared she was up in an instant. She couldn't make out who it was, but knew it wasn't Hélène.

"Who's there? Is someone out there?"

Miss Shipton. Amélie pressed herself against the wall. The sheet waved a farewell as Miss Shipton pulled it up.

"What the blazes…" Amélie heard her say, then she ran.

"You – ahoy, you there stop, STOP…"

Her voice rose to its full PE lesson level. It was more than enough to bring the guards running. Amélie dashed for the trees.

"STOP… STOP… INTRUDER…"

She ducked as she entered the wood, wary of any low-lying branches. She crouched behind a tree and looked back, trying to calm her breathing and letting her eyes grow accustomed to the dark. It was much darker in the trees.

A torch appeared at the far end of the school, its holder not in any great hurry judging by the steady beam working its way along the first-floor windows seeking the source of the bellowed alarm call.

"Time to go, Amélie," she whispered to herself. She didn't hurry through the trees, instead concentrating on where she was going, concentrating on not making any mistakes.

Occasionally she glanced back. She could hear voices, but reckoned they were still by the school building. There was the beam of a second torch. Still nobody seemed to be heading her way. Miss Shipton's loudly-earned reputation for shouting at everything did not make the guards feel the need to rush.

Amélie reached the wall and followed its path, up a small rise, down the other side, up again and then a level stretch.

Her feet squelched in the mud. This was where she had fallen. She glanced back towards the school and as she did an owl hooted nearby. She let out a squeal and at once felt stupid. A torch beam flashed at the edge of the wood. They were coming.

She placed her foot in the first hole, felt for a hand hold, found it and within a matter of moments she was at the top of the wall. She swung her leg over the top. Both torches were now in the woods. They would find no trace of her.

Amélie swung her other leg over and without hesitation jumped to the soft mossy ground on the other side. Earlier she'd conducted a daylight scouting mission, clambered to the top of the wall and looked over so she knew what to expect before hurrying back when the dinner bell rang.

"Find out as much as you can – knowledge keeps you hidden." It's what Cécile used to tell her. "It's a game of hide-and-seek, isn't it?" Amélie had replied. "In a way," said Cécile.

Chapter 23

They found her as it was getting light. She didn't notice the car, tucked close to the trees on the side of the road, until it was too late. Her first instinct was to run. She looked around; where would she go? She was already lost.

"Easy girl – Jepson sent me." A man, short and square, had stepped out of the car and faced her, leaning forward, ready to run if she did. "Now come on, we must get going before any of the search party arrive."

Amélie hung back. "You're one of Jepson's men? But how did you know I'd…"

"Ah-ha, a little bird told us you'd flown the nest. Jepson said if you were who you claimed you were, and if you were any damned good at this game then you wouldn't stay put for long. If you got out, we'd have you, if you didn't, well, you'd become jolly good at Latin and cross country runs."

He grinned at her. "So you've passed the first test, well done Miss Dreyfus. Now shall we?"

Amélie remained where she was. "First test for what?"

"I'll tell you in the car, now come on, we need to get out of here."

Amélie shook her head. "My maman always told me not to wander off with strange men. First test for what?"

The man let out an angry snort, but gave in. "Secret Service – the Secret bloody Service – it's what you wanted isn't it?"

"Will I go back to France?"

"That depends – now come on…"

The whine of an engine labouring up hill reached them.

Amélie folded her arms. "Depends on what?"

"If you complete the training – and if you don't move now you will have failed straight away."

Amélie followed as he turned and hurried to the car. She tried but failed to keep a grin from her face.

They were in the car, Amélie in the back, the man, Lieutenant Roland-Jones he said his name was, in the front next to the driver. She leaned forward, planting her arms on the seat rests.

"So who is your spy in the school? Is it Hélène? Is it?"

"Who?"

"No, I didn't think so. Nice girl, but doubt she's got the stomach for it. Must be one of the teachers? Come on tell me – we're on the same side aren't we!"

"No, Miss Dreyfus… now you should get some sleep, you've a long day ahead of you."

Amélie sat back.

"Thank you," she said. "For helping me get away from that place. I will prove worth it – I promise you that."

"We'll see, Miss," said Roland-Jones, keeping his eyes fixed out the front windscreen. He didn't seem at all convinced.

Neither, it turned out, was the man she was handed over to several hours later.

They drove into London as dawn was breaking. Amélie stared out the window; London, one of the world's great cities. That's what Maman always said.

It didn't look great that dull morning. The driver cursed – then apologised to Amélie – when they had to take a detour due to bomb damage, the broken remains of a building strewn across the road. They drove alongside the Thames for a while. In the distance Amélie glimpsed Big Ben. She wondered if she might get the chance to have a look around later, Buckingham Palace perhaps, before tutting at herself. She was not here to sightsee.

The car stopped on Oxford Street. Large X's of white tape covered shop windows, sandbags were piled here, there and everywhere, higher and higher. Lieutenant Roland-Jones opened the car door for her.

"This way," he said. He unlocked a black door tucked between two shops and ushered her in. "Third floor, number seven. They're expecting you. Codeword's 'pigeon'."

"You're not coming?"

"No – good luck, Miss Dreyfus," he said, stepping outside again. He pulled the door shut and Amélie listened to the key turning in the lock. She stood in the hallway, in the uniform of the peculiar English school she'd just run away from, in a country where she knew barely a soul, without a possession in the world apart from her necklace. Not even the clothes she wore were hers. What on earth was she doing? She fingered her necklace. What on earth was the Secret Service, whoever they really were, going to do with her?

She swallowed. Then lifted her chin towards the dark staircase. No matter; as long as it took her back to France, back to doing something to drive out the Germans, anything to help bring Maman, Papa and dear Paulie home.

She climbed the stairs, her feet echoing on the stone steps. It seemed like a normal apartment block – not as nice as hers – but a place where people made their homes. She knocked on the door of number seven. She was just about to knock again when the door opened.

"Yes?" said a small man, the look on his face suggesting she must have the wrong address.

"Um, bonjour… no, I mean hello, I'm Miss Dreyfus."

He looked her up and down. "And what of it?"

"Pigeon," she blurted out, remembering what Roland-Jones had said. It sounded loud in the stairwell, echoing upwards.

"For goodness sake, girl," said the man and pulled her into the apartment.

He pointed down the corridor and shut the door. With a series of grunts he directed her into a room overlooking Oxford Street and into a hard-backed chair facing a small table. Her host took a chair on the other side of the table and opened a brown folder.

"Miss Dreyfus," he read, "Miss Amélie Dreyfus. Born Paris – that right?"

"Yes," she said and leaned forward to see what else was written about her. There was a snatched photograph of her, in her English school uniform. The man leaned forward too and put his arm across the top of the folder as if she were trying to cheat in a school test.

She sat back. "Good," he said, and sat back too.

"What is your name?" she said. She knew she wouldn't get an answer.

"I'll ask the questions, thank you, Miss Dreyfus. Now, are you fluent in French?"

"I beg your pardon?"

"Do… you… speak… French?" He spoke in that particular way English people use when talking to foreigners, as if they suspect the world beyond the Channel to be full of people less intelligent than them.

"I am French."

"I see. So you speak French?"

"So I speak French."

He wrote something in her folder.

"Good," he said. "And you claim you were a courier for a Resistance group?"

"I don't claim – I was." Amélie stood up. "Look, what is this? I've not come here to be treated like a liar or… or a child. I got one of your precious pilots out of France, I escaped the Gestapo, I told you about a traitor…"

"Sit down, please, Miss Dreyfus, getting all French about this and hot under the collar is not going to help anyone."

Amélie turned and strode to the door. "Good morning, Monsieur Whatever Your Name. I'm going now."

"Wait…" The man stood up, the chair legs scraping on the wooden floor. "How do we know you're not the traitor?"

Amélie stopped, her hand on the door handle.

"The Gestapo are clever, and cruel. It would be just like them to force you to work for them, betray your network to save yourself or somebody you care for… this game of ours is not played by the book. There is no book…"

He sat down again and pulled his chair in. "It is down to me, and me alone, to determine whether Amélie Dreyfus is a double agent, who has already betrayed an entire network. There are two policemen waiting in the kitchen across the hall, both armed – a word from me and you will be taken to Holloway prison. We are not treating you like a child. Do you understand?"

He smoothed down his thinning hair, returning a loose strand to its proper place. Amélie sat down.

"Good," he said.

For the next hour he asked Amélie question after question, and then the same questions again, picking over her answers, asking her about Cécile, about Alain, about Raymond. About how she met them, what she did for them, the pilots who were captured, who was at fault for that? "Raymond," she said and stared hard at the man. What about Tony? Could he be a spy perhaps? A plant. Everyone

175

was a suspect. Round and round they went. Her mouth was dry and she felt light-headed.

"Good," said the man, breaking a period of silence. He shut the folder.

"Good?" wondered Amélie.

"Yes. You've convinced me."

"So what happens now?"

"To you?"

"Oui."

"Well you, Miss Dreyfus… we're sending you back to school."

Chapter 24

Amélie's spirits lifted a little when Jepson appeared at the apartment and whisked her off for lunch. She liked him, not least because he'd told her his name. But they soon drooped as she stared at a plate of grey fish, watery mashed potato and something green and slimy.

"I will not go back to school," she said, staring hard at Jepson.

"School? Gosh, no, you've made that quite clear, old girl."

"Am I going home?"

"Home..."

Amélie was beginning to find it increasingly difficult to work out what was true and what was false in this new world.

"No, not yet."

"Well, where am I going?"

"You'll see, top secret location – drive you down there after lunch, now come on eat up, before it gets cold."

Jepson drove fast, making Amélie's tummy leap and dive over every hump and round every corner. London, with its barrage balloons, sandbags and bomb-damaged houses, looked much more at war than the Paris she'd left behind. Outside the city they saw few cars – petrol was hard to come by – and soon pulled up outside a large gate topped with barbed wire.

Three soldiers, rifles slung over shoulders, emerged from a wooden hut on the side of the road. Two stood in front of the gate while the other examined Jepson's papers and a pass Amélie had been given before leaving the apartment.

The gate squealed as it was pushed open. It clanged shut behind them, a sound that made Amélie feel uncomfortable.

"What is this place?"

Jepson said nothing.

The drive meandered through rolling grounds before revealing a large mansion that had seen better days. It was a house that looked weary. Much of it was covered with ivy, at the far end two windows were boarded up. The flower beds that ran along the front were filled with weeds and the lawn that led away from the side of the house needed a good cut.

"Here we are then," said Jepson. "Your home for the next… well, the next while."

"What is this place?" repeated Amélie, stepping out of the car.

"Actually, it is a school… of sorts," said Jepson as the large front door, painted a dull, military-looking green, opened and a tall, sturdy woman dressed in a tweed suit came down the steps. A large dog, its tail wagging, followed her.

"Welcome, welcome," said the woman, her arms open.

"This," said Jepson, waving his hand at the house, "is Wanborough Manor – our school…" Amélie frowned at the word, Jepson paused and grinned at her… "our school for spies."

The dog, its tail waving a frantic greeting, galloped across the gravel and bounded up to Amélie. She put her hand out. Labrador: faithful and reliable, good with children…

"This," continued Jepson, "is Gulliver."

Amélie stroked the dog and it nuzzled against her. She watched the woman approach – she looked as if she'd be rather harder to win over than Gulliver.

"And this," said Jepson, "is the Headmistress."

"Thank you, Captain Jepson," she said, taking Amélie's hand and pumping it in a vigorous hello. "Actually, it's Mrs Appleblossom. Welcome to Wanborough Manor – we hope you won't be happy here because if you are we're not doing our jobs properly."

She unleashed a ferocious grin at Amélie and gestured for her to enter the Manor.

"Best of luck, old girl," said Jepson. "Best learn the ropes quickly."

Her school uniform was swapped for an itchy military uniform, a khaki shirt (too big) and jacket (too big) with matching trousers (too big). Everywhere she went she billowed.

She was given another new name. For the duration of her training she would be June (they liked to name female recruits after months or seasons). As promised there were none of the usual school rules at Wanborough Manor but plenty of ropes to learn, real and imaginary.

The real ropes were round the back of the Manor, an assault course which the dozen spies-in-training had to complete once a day, and always faster than the day before. Throughout they were shouted at by a small and always angry sergeant with a tuneful Welsh accent. He sounded like he was about to burst into song as he yelled abuse at them while they climbed and crawled and scrambled around the muddy course.

The imaginary ropes were even harder to workout. Trust

no-one was the school motto, apart from Mrs Appleblossom – which Amélie presumed was a codename because nothing in this world was what it seemed. Certainly not the other 11 pupils.

Pupils were encouraged to steal, lie and cheat. Normal rules were there to be broken. If a pupil left a pen or pencil, notebook or even a biscuit lying around, the others whisked it away.

"From now on you live life on the edge," instructed Mrs Appleblossom. "You are not bound by rules. Learn to take, take what's useful, what's disruptive, if someone has a lucky charm take it, anything to make the enemy's existence more difficult, more uncomfortable. You are here to learn to live – for the duration of this war – outside normal rules.

"You are excused because you will be against a ruthless enemy, who will stop at nothing to destroy you. Learn to live on the edge, seek out that edge and take it – no matter what. Lives depend on it."

There was one rule. Only French could be spoken and that suited Amélie down to the ground. Their French teacher, an old Englishwoman with the tightest bun Amélie had ever seen – it made her look permanently surprised – would call Amélie to the front of the class to repeat words or phrases the others struggled with.

And the others? Seven men and four women, all several years older than Amélie and they didn't take kindly to being shown up by a girl. It meant they did little to help her when she struggled with Morse code lessons – they were taught code and how to use a radio. Amélie was forever getting her dots and dashes muddled up. To the amusement of the others.

Amélie got her own back by hiding their things. She had arrived with nothing but her necklace which she never removed. She had become used to living with nothing, so had nothing for the others to pinch. She could not bring herself to steal (anything taken had to be delivered to Mrs Appleblossom's office). It felt wrong, and so she settled for hiding her fellow pupils' belongings and then 'discovering' them again after allowing time for a frantic search.

One Sunday morning Amélie 'found' April's good shoes, the ones she kept in case they were ever allowed a day out. April was so relieved to have them back she took Amélie under her wing. At first Amélie felt guilty, but then she reasoned she was just doing what she would have to when she got to back to Paris – winning the support of someone she needed by whatever means possible. Besides she liked April.

It was good to have someone to sit next to at dinner and

182

chat with in the evenings, even if April did talk an awful lot about boys. Her favourites were RAF pilots. "I know a pilot, Tony," said Amélie.

"Why you dark horse," exclaimed April – she did a lot of exclaiming, she was that sort of person. "How on earth, June? Do tell."

"Well, I got him..." Amélie's voice trailed off. She shouldn't be talking about this. They'd been ordered never to tell anyone at the school about their previous lives. Careless talk really could cost lives, as the posters warned. The rumour was one of their number was a plant, someone put there by the Secret Service to try and trick them into making a mistake, saying something they shouldn't. And if they did they would be expelled.

"Oh nothing," said Amélie. April smiled at her and launched into a story of a disastrous dinner with a Royal Navy captain that involved an air-raid, an escaped horse, a pile of dung that escaped from the escaped horse and the captain's whiter-than-white uniform.

The weeks passed and they learnt their new trade. How to write in code, how to make a secret exchange with a fellow agent, how to spot if you were being followed and how to shake off any followers.

They were given civilian clothes and taken into the nearest

town to practice, two pupils as agents given a meeting place to exchange a message, the other ten sent to hunt them down. One week they were taken in one at a time and told the local police and Home Guard had been given their pictures and ordered to arrest them. Amélie only escaped by darting into a school playground and disappearing among the oldest children enjoying their break – teachers and pupils were used to evacuees arriving by the day so assumed she was where she was supposed to be.

Sometimes it did feel like a game, especially when a large dressing-up box was put in the middle of the teaching room one morning. A woman came with the box, a well-dressed woman who they were told worked for a famous fashion magazine. She showed them how to dress-up and change their appearance – put on a hat with a wide brim, or a pair of glasses, gloves, or brush your hair a different way; anything to change the way you look. It might buy a few extra minutes, added the instructor, and make the difference between life and death.

So they learnt the dos-and-don'ts of living in occupied France, the best places to meet, the places to avoid, and every morning that slog over the assault course while the sergeant assaulted their ears.

Even in the evening, when they would sprawl in easy

chairs and listen to records on the gramophone, they had to be on their guard, keeping an eye on the others, watching what they said.

One night a small Scotsman, who looked like he'd been chewed up by life, put on a jazz record. Amélie recognised it at once. It was one of Paulie's favourites. She stood up and crossed to the window, turning her back on the others. The Scotsman began to whistle the tune. Amélie felt a tear well up in her right eye. Paulie... where was he?

"June?" April was standing behind her. "Are you all right?"

Amélie brushed a hand over her eye, getting rid of the tear.

"Yes," she said, turning and forcing a smile.

"Memories?" said April.

"Yes," said Amélie.

Chapter 25

Mrs Appleblossom was seated behind a large desk. She was the sort of person who suited a large desk.

"Now then," she announced, her voice as decisive as ever, "June…"

She was studying a familiar brown folder, although since Amélie had last set eyes on it its contents had multiplied.

"June… French, excellent – jolly good – losing a pursuer, good, following a target, good, disguise, good, coding, passable, morse, ah, I see."

She shut the folder with a firm slap and studied Amélie. Amélie returned her gaze.

"Righto," said Mrs Appleblossom. "You're a hard one to read, Miss June. Which, in our line of work, is no bad thing."

Out the large window behind Mrs Appleblossom's

desk a truck drew up, its heavy wheels crunching on the gravel. The driver leapt down from the cabin and opened the back.

"Ah," said Mrs Appleblossom, "the station truck." She checked her watch. "In plenty of time too, good, good…"

She studied Amélie again. "I decide whether you should be on that truck, June. Do you know where it's going?"

Amélie had an idea, April had told her the rumours of what the next stage of training involved. "Blowing things up – yippee!" she'd whispered to Amélie at dinner a couple of nights before.

"No," said Amélie to Mrs Appleblossom.

"Scotland, well, to the station where the train will take my newest Wanborough graduates to Scotland."

She stared at Amélie.

"I don't think you're ready to go with them."

"What? No…"

"Yes – there's your morse code, that's reason enough to keep you here longer. But it's not only that… how old are you, Amélie?"

It was the first time Mrs Appleblossom had called her by her first name, her real first name.

"Nearly 18, I'm nearly 18, old enough to be a soldier."

"Are you?"

"Yes – why would I lie?"

Mrs Appleblossom raised a doubting eyebrow and opened the folder again.

"Nearly 18 you say – then it must nearly be your birthday." She studied the top page in the folder. "There's no date of birth here is there... typical men to forget your birthday. When is your birthday?"

She looked up again as she asked the question. Amélie looked down. She could feel Mrs Appleblossom's appraising eyes on her.

"The 18th of November."

"Yes, so soon... what year were you born?"

"Um, 19... 19..." Amélie's mind whirred trying to do the sum. She was never very good at maths. If she was going to be 18 in 1943, taking away 17 and...

"You will stay here for the time being – you are too young, my dear."

"But I must go – I must go home." Amélie stood up suddenly; Mrs Appleblossom tilted her head to one side.

"Why?" she said.

"Because..." Amélie had told nobody about Maman and Papa and Paulie. Certainly not the mouse man who'd interrogated her in Oxford Street but not even Cécile. She didn't want anyone knowing everything about her. She wanted to keep something for herself; something of herself from them.

"My mother, and my father… the Germans took them."

"I see… they were in the Resistance too?"

"No."

"Well, why did they take them?"

"They are… we are Jewish."

"I see."

"And I will do everything I can to get them back, anything…"

"And to avenge them?"

"Um, yes."

"I see." Mrs Appleblossom stood up and came round to the front of the desk. She put a hand on Amélie's arm. "Well, I'm afraid that is another reason to keep you here – our job is not about revenge. We must be cold and dispassionate, not hot headed – that clouds judgement."

"But I… I did this job you talk about – I was… I am in the Resistance, I know how to outfox the Germans…"

"And what happened to your network?"

The question hung between them. Amélie heard the roaring in her ears, anger swelled inside her. She bit her tongue, actually bit it to stop herself opening her mouth.

"Listen," said Mrs Appleblossom. "Stay here for another

year – help teach the pupils French, real French, the language used on the streets of Paris, the slang. It's an important job – if you teach them well it can make the difference between life and death."

"After a year?"

"Well, we'll see – we'll review how well you've done. And then maybe… maybe you will be sent to France."

Amélie nodded, not trusting herself to say another word. She turned and hurried towards the door only to be halted by a loud hiss of steam from outside. Through the window she could see it rising from beneath the truck's bonnet.

"Ah," said Mrs Appleblossom, "looks like nobody will be going to Scotland today anyway."

Which, it turned out, was extremely fortunate for Amélie.

She went to bed straight after dinner, brushing away April's attempts to discover what the matter was.

In recent months Amélie had become a light sleeper. It showed, she was convinced, how ready she was to be a spy. The slightest noise woke her. It had begun in Paris where every night came with the chance she might be hauled from her sleep by the Gestapo.

So it was a little after two o'clock that something, a whisper of the night, woke her. The curtain to the woman's dorm had not been closed properly, nor the blackout put up, and the light of the moon shone into the room. Amélie lay stock still. There was someone in the room – there were the other female trainees of course, but she could sense someone else, someone who didn't belong there.

There was a mumble from the bed next to hers, May muttering something in her sleep. Was that what had woken Amélie? She lay and listened.

A creak of a floorboard. There… she saw her, or him. He was coming into the gap between her bed and May's, leaning towards May…

"Yaaaaarrrrgghhhh," yelled Amélie – shouting was a good way of confusing an attacker and alerting everyone else – and launched herself at the intruder.

She crashed into him and the two of them tumbled onto May's bed. May, by everyone's reckoning the toughest agent, male or female, to pass through Wanborough Hall, sat up in bed and swung her fist at the intruder.

"The blanket," said Amélie, "wrap him in the blanket."

The fight had already been knocked out of the intruder by May's weighty right hook and within a couple of minutes they'd swaddled him in her blanket and were both sitting on him. The rest of the dorm was awake, April turned on the light.

"Let's see who he is then," she said as the door opened

and a fully-dressed Mrs Appleblossom – did she ever sleep? wondered Amélie – strode in.

"What on earth have you done to Mr Loucky?"

Mr Loucky was one of the instructors, a code teacher who fussed about every tiny detail. Amélie didn't like him. She pulled back the blanket to check. Mr Loucky stared back at her, one of his eyes already blackening thanks to May's thunderbolt.

They climbed off him and helped him to his feet. His thinning hair stuck out at all angles making him look like a scarecrow. More like a scared crow, thought Amélie taking in his black polo neck and black trousers – his uniform for creeping around in the dark – and grinned at her own joke.

"What is so amusing, Miss June?" asked Mrs Appleblossom.

"Er, nothing."

"An explanation, please," barked Mrs Appleblossom.

Amélie told her about waking up to spot an intruder but Mrs Appleblossom interrupted her. "Mr Loucky was simply doing his job."

"What?"

"Yes – it is Mr Loucky's unfortunate task to skulk around the bedrooms at night checking for sleep talkers."

"I don't understand," said April.

Mrs Appleblossom shook her head. "It's really quite simple – you may all be fluent in French and spend all day talking French. But what about when you're asleep? If you sleep talk it will be in English, and that is something we cannot risk for an agent being sent to France.

"It's not only your lives at stake – this is a good time to remind you before you leave in the morning. One mistake by any of you can cost many, many lives. You must think of everything, and we must think of everything before we let any of you go.

"Well, Mr Loucky?"

He nodded. "Same again, I'm afraid."

"What do you suggest?"

He shook his head.

"Very well," said Mrs Appleblossom. "Miss May – you will not be going. Not yet, not until we sort out your problem."

"But…" began May.

"This is not the first time, Miss May, I'm afraid – we'll talk to the doctors, find a way."

"If you say so," said May, her face falling as she spoke.

"I do – now back to sleep, ladies," said Mrs Appleblossom, returning to the door. "Long journey ahead of you tomorrow."

Her hand hovered over the light switch.

"Oh and Miss June – you will be going." She flicked the switch. "I promised them four female agents and they shall have four female agents. Don't let me down."

Spotting the open curtain, she crossed the room, pulled down the blackout curtain with a brisk 'tsk' and tugged the real curtain shut too. When she closed the door behind her the dorm was dark.

"Sorry," whispered Amélie into the darkness. May sighed and turned over. Amélie closed her eyes, a smile on her face.

Chapter 26

Amélie glanced at the sky. It wasn't easy to work out where the sun was but she had a pretty good idea. She shivered and turned the compass until it was lined up with the map. She studied the map. She was on time, on course and, so far, unseen.

She pulled her woollen commando hat off and scratched round her head. The itch spread into her hair and she ran her fingers through it rubbing her scalp. It was horrible the hat – smelt of all the previous wearers no matter how many times she washed it – but it was green and helped her blend into the landscape, even if most of the land was brown.

What was it about Britain? Brown food in England morning, noon and night and now Scotland, the world's brownest country. She'd no idea there could be so many shades of brown.

She folded up the map and returned it to her pack, alongside the water bottle – even the burn water she'd re-filled her bottle with had a tinge of brown (from the peaty ground). The pack held camouflage paint for her face, an emergency ration pack chocolate bar and a quarter of a loaf of bread she'd removed from the kitchen when no-one was looking the morning they were sent off on their mission.

It began with the trainee agents dropped one by one from a lorry on a bleak, wind-swept moor. Eight of them remained – two of the men had broken limbs, one arm, one leg, during the six weeks they'd spent at Arisaig, a top-secret camp hidden away in the Highlands.

The two-day mission had to be completed by midnight, so they were sternly instructed, with a rendezvous at a cottage on a small island just off the mainland. The wilderness they had to cross was patrolled by soldiers and the instructors. Getting caught meant a fail, failing to get to the cottage in time meant a fail and failure meant a return to Wanborough Manor, an outcome that did not bear thinking about.

Amélie took the map out and studied it once more – just to be sure. She'd never read a map without streets on it before she arrived at Arisaig, where the agents were housed in another large and crumbling old mansion. The chill winds, not to mention the regular rain and occasional snow squalls of a Scottish winter, meant warmth was even more difficult to come by than a decent meal.

Amélie was actually warmest when she was out and about, learning how to wrestle an opponent to the ground or pin them to the wall, how to hide and how to build a shelter, although she wasn't sure what use that would be in Paris. Nevertheless to her city-girl surprise she found she was at home in this wild place. Apart from April, the others still had little time for her, nicknaming her the Bairn – the Scottish word for baby one of the instructors told her – and leaving her alone each evening in the big house while they trooped down to the bottom of the drive where the soldiers who guarded the secret base had set up a pub in one of the estate workers' cottages.

Amélie stayed in her room, huddled under her blankets. Or pulled an armchair as close to the big fire in the living room as she could – having tossed on every log stacked at the side of the fireplace (the 'grown-ups' could face the cold when they got back). She read old books from the library about forgotten battles and long-gone people, as well as about the animals and plants and trees that called this harsh land home. There was one book, old and ignored, some of its pages merged together with damp, about the estate itself, the land, islands and seashore around the big house. This one she studied with particular interest.

One night, feeling like the class swot, she spread her map alongside the one in the front of the estate book and compared the two. She made several thick pencil markings on her map and slept well that night, pleased with herself.

Other nights she stayed awake staring into the dark. Home whispered to her, thoughts of Maman made her happy and then sad and it was the sadness that stuck to her. She began to draw, mapping the apartment, marking carefully where each piece of furniture was, even each picture and decoration – Maman liked her knick-knacks. Before the others returned from the pub she would hide the drawings beneath her mattress.

She broke off a piece of bread and chewed it carefully as she watched, some way below, April trudging along a path down the glen. April was still friendly, but less so when others were around. Amélie had been blamed for taking May's place. Everyone liked May and there were rumours, April told her, that Amélie set up the whole Mr Loucky incident to get herself to Scotland.

"How?" said Amélie. April shrugged, and burped. She'd drunk several pints of beer.

For a while Amélie watched April head along the track. She didn't mind being alone. Well, she did but was prepared to put up with it if it meant getting back home.

Besides if April was going to follow the path to the coast she would almost certainly blunder into whatever trap the instructors were setting, and that distraction would improve Amélie's chances of making the rendezvous. Make the rendezvous and she was as good as on the boat home.

She scanned the path and the brown glen beyond. She should have brought binoculars, 'borrowed' the old pair from where they hung in the hall. She cursed herself under her breath, but kept her eyes on her surroundings. Movement or colour (apart from brown) that's what she was looking for, anything that suggested a human presence.

Nothing caught her eye so she swallowed the last of the bread (brown of course), buckled her pack and swung it on to her back. She climbed, scrabbling over rocks and grabbing handfuls of heather to help her up the steeper parts. She moved as quickly as she could – anyone on lookout would spot her; but they would spot her no matter what speed she went. The faster she was over the summit and down the other side the better.

Another couple of hours and she was at the top, peering

cautiously over the edge. It was like looking down on a painting. The sea glittered in the early afternoon sunshine. She reckoned she had a couple of hours of daylight left.

Below her lay the island, their target. She studied it. Looking from above allowed her to pick out the cottage where they were to meet, and spot the men hiding above the path leading towards the cottage from the island's jetty.

She switched her attention to the green, blue, grey brush stroke of sea that separated the island from the mainland. The island sat at an angle, as though its southern end was anchored and the north had drifted further out.

Back on the mainland, she saw the track curve round a small hill and end where a stone pier jutted out towards the island. Tied to the pier were three rowing boats, bobbing on the gentle waves. There were other small boats pulled up on the shoreline beyond the jetty, tempting targets. In a boat it would take no time at all to make the island.

The crossing was short. Little more than a couple of lengths of a swimming pool away the island jetty pointed back towards the mainland. There was a larger boat tied alongside.

A small cliff rose above the crossing point on the mainland, offering commanding views back down the track and over the pier, and sure enough Amélie spotted a flicker of movement. Someone, probably several someones, were waiting on the cliff top.

Amélie checked her watch – she was on time – slipped over the ridge and began her descent. She went slowly this time; it was easier to fall going down. She was counting on little attention being paid to the hillside and even if one of the Someones did spot her they would assume she was heading for the crossing point.

She wasn't. She was making for a small beach and on its golden sands she found what she was looking for, wood and rope – the sea spitting out man's rubbish. She lashed several pieces of driftwood together, watching the tide all the time. It was beginning to go out. She had to hurry.

And she had to hope the estate book was right. Once upon a long time ago, she'd read with growing interest one dark and stormy night, the clan chief had been looking to hide his cattle from the Red Coats, the King's soldiers out to plunder and rob. There was a hidden cave on the far side of the island, reached only at low tide, but the crossing point was guarded by the Red Coats.

So one evening, from this very beach, the clan chief and a handful of men swam the cows out towards the far end of the island, trusting in what he'd been told by a wise woman (or witch some might have called her). Because of the peculiarities of the seabed and the movement of the tide, a man or cow, or teenage girl, could be all but swept out to sea and then flung back into the small bay just beyond the island's northern tip. If they got their tide timings right.

Amélie smeared camouflage paint across her cheeks and forehead, undressed to her underwear, put her clothes in her pack and buckled it tight, changed her mind, took out the chocolate bar and broke off a couple of chunks which she swallowed. She put the pack on the small raft and pushed it into the sea. She gasped at the cold but did not hesitate. She pushed again and then dropped herself into the water.

She kicked out, pointing the raft beyond the island, out to sea. If this went wrong… if she had read the tide times wrong… She kicked again and felt herself being taken. The retreating tide had her. She gripped tight to the raft and kept kicking.

The light was disappearing. If anyone was watching from the island they would see a chunk of driftwood being swept into the ocean, next stop Greenland or maybe America.

It happened more quickly than Amélie could have hoped for, and exactly as written in the old book in the hall library. Just beyond where the island's northern tip stretched into the sea, the land fell away beneath the waves and then rose again in a thin stack of rock almost to the surface.

The sea swirled around this point, not quite a whirlpool but when the tide was right it created enough of a whirl to tug you into the small bay. Amélie rode her luck – and the currents. It felt like a fairground ride. Only colder. A lot colder. Soon she was shivering on the beach as she used her shirt to dry herself.

By the time she reached the cottage her teeth were chattering. Major Brown, the chief instructor, was sitting alone at the kitchen table when she lifted the latch and walked in. His eyebrows rose as if on a piece of string.

"Now that's a damned surprise," he said in his deep Highland voice. For a moment she thought he was the old clan chief.

She felt the warmth of the room hug her. It was too much. Her head felt heavy. The room started to spin.

"I…" she said and it went black.

Chapter 27

"Très bien," said April when Amélie opened the heavy dining room door and peaked round. Everyone was there, the seven remaining would-be agents, seated around the large table, plates piled with scrambled eggs and toast. There was jam on the table – a real treat – and bowls of autumn raspberries picked from the hall's over-grown gardens. A fire cackled and spat, competing with the rattle of rain on the large windows.

"Jolly well done," continued April, beaming at Amélie. "Come, eat… it's scrummy and you must be starving, you've been asleep for a whole day."

"Have I?" wondered Amélie. She still felt tired, and a little light-headed.

"June, here… there's a space here." Coventry stood up – the men were called after English towns and cities – and gestured at the place next to him. They were the first words he'd ever spoken to her.

"Yes," said April, coming to the door and escorting Amélie into the room as though she'd seen her first and was determined to claim the girl for herself. "You have a seat and I'll bring you some eggs."

"And," said Hereford, "you simply must tell us how you did it. First one home – the Bairn goes to the top of the class. Brown is being rather coy about it, says it's your secret to tell."

Amélie sat down as April placed a plate in front of her. The smell of the scrambled eggs flicked a switch inside and hunger surged through her.

"Oh, and he wants to see you," said April, returning to her place. "After breakfast, in his office."

"Major Brown?"

Two platefuls of scrambled egg on toast, four extra slices of toast with raspberry jam, a handful of raspberries and three cups of sugary tea later, Amélie mounted the stairs to Major Brown's office. She felt a glow inside, and not just because her stomach was full. After the triumph of the island exercise, a good sleep and an even better breakfast she was ready for whatever the Major could throw at her. At least she thought she was.

Brown's office had once been the laird's study. The fire was lit and Brown sat to one side of it. He was wearing a kilt. Next to him a large brown paper package sat on a table.

"Ah, the birthday girl" he said, his voice as deep and comforting as the armchair he was embedded in. He waved her to a matching armchair on the other side of the fire, "Many happy returns – enjoy the special breakfast did you?"

"My birthday?"

"Yes." He patted the folder on his lap – her file.

"Yes, of course."

"November the 18th – ah, no year, so what year was it…"

"1925," said Amélie, "18th November, 1925 – in Paris."

"Paris, yes, exactly – that's why… wait, hang on, birthday first – a present."

He threw the parcel on to the floor in front of her chair. "Open it."

Amélie tugged at the string and the paper opened to reveal a beret, a jacket and a skirt all in the same dull brown colour.

"Your uniform, Miss Dreyfus – when you leave here to

re-join the outside world you will be part of the First Aid Nursery Yeomanry, it's what all female agents join as a cover story. You will receive a salary of £300 per annum."

"A salary?"

"Yes, you're working for us from now on."

"Us?"

"The British government. Just for the war you understand – then when we've thrown the Nazis out of France you can go back to being... well, whatever you were before all this began."

Amélie opened her mouth. Brown raised his hand.

"I don't need to know that," he said. "Look, to tell the truth we're in trouble in Paris. So it's a stroke of luck that you're now 18 and old enough to be sent overseas..."

He coughed. Amélie studied the pattern of flames in the fireplace. Brown cleared his throat.

"Right, um... yes, quite... we need good people in Paris, the very best French speakers, as soon as possible. You'll receive a full briefing when you get to London."

"I'm going back to Paris?"

"Yes, it means you won't complete the training here – no blowing stuff up for you I'm afraid Miss Dreyfus – but that's not what's needed in Paris anyway."

"I'm going home?"

"It's your choice – you can say no. But you have done well here, the unarmed combat was fine, your mapwork was good and of course your mission was outstanding. You are resourceful, young lady."

He studied her. "Well, what am I to tell our high and mighties down in London?"

Amélie grinned at him. "Tell them I'm going home."

Everything happened briskly from then, beginning with Major Brown striding to his desk, picking up the telephone and dialling. The whirrrr of the dial returning to its place after each number sounded loud to Amélie.

"She'll do it," said Brown. He looked at his watch. "Aye, she can make that if she hurries."

Packing took no time because she had next to nothing to pack. She changed into the uniform, which felt baggy on her and pulled on the cap which sat awkwardly on her ears. She took her drawings of home down to the dining room, now empty, and dropped them in the fire.

"Wufff," said each sheet as it caught light and curled into ashes.

It was late by the time she arrived in London – in the dining car she'd been served something called Brown Soup, which tasted exactly as she expected – but the station was still busy.

"June?"

She jumped. She hadn't noticed the man approach her. She nodded.

"Come with me," he said and set off through the station at a brisk pace.

Outside a taxi drew up without the man even lifting a finger. He opened the door and ushered Amélie inside. The driver pulled away without even asking for an address.

"Where are we going?"

"No questions please, miss," said the man and turned away from her to stare out the window at the dark streets – the blackout was in place. There was nothing to see.

They stopped in a quiet street. "Orchard Park," said the driver. The man led her to a door and, just as when she'd first arrived in London, opened it and locked it once she was inside. The third-floor flat she entered this time was night-and-day different. It was busy for a start. A woman opened the door.

"Come in, darling," she said. "I'm Vera Atkins, I play mother to our female agents. I'm afraid, darling, we're in a bit of a rush with you so we won't have much of a chance to get to know each other – we'll have time for a chat on the way to the airfield tomorrow…"

She glanced up at the clock in the hall. "Tonight rather.

Let's get you a bed then we'll have you up for a briefing and final run through first thing. Follow me, darling…"

She poked her head round the first door. "She's here," she said and closed it again. "The boss, you'll meet him in the morning, terribly busy man." She threw her words over her shoulder at Amélie.

"Here we are – you can have the Round Room. Everything should be there for you – pair of clean jim-jams, wash things, towel – bathroom across the hall there."

"Excuse me," said Amélie, standing in the doorway and looking at a room in which every piece of furniture, including the bed, was round. "What are jim-jams?"

"Of course, I forgot. Pyjamas, my darling – pyjamas. Meant for a chap I'm afraid but they'll do for you for the one night."

With that she spun on her heel and returned to the room where the boss was. There was a brief rumble of voices and then the door clicked shut.

Amélie crossed the hall and opened the bathroom door. It was covered floor to ceiling in black tiles and dominated by a large, black-tiled, bathtub. A man, fully clothed in a dark suit and bow tie – he looked like he'd come from a night at the opera – lay in the empty bath. He was studying a map.

"Oh, frightfully sorry," he said, standing up and stepping out of the bath. He still had his shoes on. He looked both young and old, a young man who'd seen too much war perhaps. His dark hair was swept back from his forehead apart from a strand that had worked itself loose. He also had a pencil-thin moustache, which made him look, thought Amélie, not British at all.

Yet he could not have sounded more English if he'd tried. He spoke like the announcer who read the news on the wireless. "Quietest place in this madhouse, best spot for a bit of work."

He looked at her. "You must be the French girl." He put a hand out. "Good to have you on board." She shook his hand. "I'll leave you to, um, to… yes, I'll leave. Chin, chin."

Amélie watched him head further down the corridor – the flat seemed to go on forever – he opened another door. "Hello, George," he said. "Mind if I join you?"

What on earth, wondered Amélie as she retreated to her room, have I got myself into? She shut her door. From outside there was the growl of a car making slow progress down the street. She heard footsteps come down the corridor. They stopped outside her room. She waited, nothing. She crossed to her door and opened it. There was no-one there.

Chapter 28

"Righto… here," said Vera Atkins, patting a small pile of clothes, "is what you'll wear for your journey. Check the labels before you put them on – be trebly sure they're all French. Can't have you turning up in France wearing a skirt from Selfridges, can we? You French even sew buttons on differently – which is not something I ever expected to learn but there we are…"

Vera moved on round the large table that filled the middle of the room. Once it would have been the living room with its tall windows and happy wallpaper. A couple of straight-backed armchairs pushed back against the wall suggested brighter days gone by.

Amélie's mind was whirring. She'd been woken early by a sharp knock on the door to find Vera bearing a breakfast tray, a boiled egg, toast cut into soldiers, an odd

English custom, Amélie decided, and a cup of strong, sweet tea.

Vera watched her as she ate, sitting up in bed like she was ill and Maman had brought her breakfast in bed. Amélie told Vera about the man in the bathroom.

"Bother him," said Vera.

"Who was he?"

"You don't need to know," said Vera. There was a sharpness to her tone. It scared Amélie, scared her for what she was getting herself into.

"Not dunking?"

"I'm sorry?"

"The soldiers – in your egg, delicious."

"I… um…"

"The game you're joining," interrupted Vera. Her voice softened and she took hold of one of Amélie's hands. A game, thought Amélie, why do they keep calling it a game. But she liked it that Vera held her hand.

"This game is full of secrets and secrets it's better for you not know. Just in case… in case, well, never mind – you eat up, get yourself dressed and come and find me in the room at the end of the hall. We'll get you all kitted out. Tell you what's what… and what's not."

Vera let out a sharp laugh. She smiled at Amélie. "We'll

keep you busy, my darling, don't you worry. No time to think. Then a nice lunch before we head off – the Ritz I think. Ever been to the Ritz?"

"No," said Amélie.

"What about the Ritz in Paris then?"

Amélie shook her head. "I'll tell you what then, when this blasted war is won I will come to Paris and take you for lunch at your Ritz. Shall we?"

"Yes," said Amélie. "I'd like that."

As she dressed she decided she would bring Paulie to this lunch as well – he would enjoy the drama of this new world she was becoming part of, and he'd love the Ritz.

"Amélie…"

Amélie looked up from the pile of clothes. She was finding it difficult to concentrate. So much to take in.

"You must pay attention, my darling," said Vera. "Detail is everything."

Vera placed a hand on a dark grey suitcase that lay on the table. "Changes of clothes. Wrapped in your 'dirty' underwear – you see, my darling, if you've been travelling you will have some dirty clothes in your bag… detail, detail. Anyway, wrapped in a pair of dirty bloomers is a spare crystal for your network's radio set."

She clicked open the case and lifted the lid.

"Hidden in the lining is a thousand francs – you will be told what to do with it in the briefing – and a spare set of papers. When you get to your accommodation, you must hide the papers. Any sign of trouble, an inquisitive Boche, abandon the suitcase – you are more important. It's trickier to replace an agent than a thousand francs and some dirty bloomers. Understand?"

"Yes," said Amélie.

"Good," said Vera. She shut the suitcase. "You will also have a handbag with your papers and other bits and pieces any woman would carry. Ah, remind me to make out a café bill – we have some from the Café Mabilon in Paris. You know it? We'll scrumple that up and leave it at the bottom of your bag."

At the far end of the table four bowls were filled with what looked like dirt. "What's that?"

"Ah," said Vera, "now we do think this is clever. That is dirt, dust, sand from different areas of France. What we do is empty some in your bag or rub it onto your shoes, trouser turn ups, pockets, whatever… so if your papers say you've come from Marseille your pockets will say that too. You see different areas of France have different colours in the soil – look at the paintings, you can see that.

"Detail… it can save your life because no matter how

215

clever you are – and you're never as clever as you think you are – there will be a German or a policeman who is cleverer. It is easier to be the hunter than the hunted – for a start there are many more hunters. Righto, we're done in here I think… follow me."

She led Amélie back down the corridor, to the room where the boss was.

"Buckmaster," said the man behind the desk, getting up to shake Amélie's hand and gesture her into a seat in front of the desk. "Maurice Buckmaster."

"The man in charge," added Vera, "le grand fromage…"

She smiled at Amélie, who couldn't see a big cheese anywhere in the room. Sometimes the British baffled her.

Buckmaster shook his head. "Thank you, Vera." He opened a drawer in his desk and took out a folder, laid it on the desktop and flicked it open. He took an identity card and slid it over to Amélie followed by two pieces of papers.

"Your ID card and travel permits – they'll see you from Tours to Paris. You are a student, studying architecture, you've been to Tours to see the cathedral. One of the finest examples of Gothic architecture in the whole of France I believe."

He opened another drawer and removed an envelope. "Money – enough to get you to Paris and for any immediate expenses but not enough to arouse suspicion should the Germans stop you. What else…

"Yes, your code name is Chocolat. This is how it will work…"

Buckmaster's voice was soft. Amélie listened, listened as hard as she could. It was difficult when her mind wouldn't stop spinning. Code name Chocolat, the name on her papers Clémentine Riffaud, another new name, another her. Could she be a Clémentine? She must remember who she was supposed to be, as well as who she really was. Her head was spinning so much she feared her memory might fly out an ear and Amélie, the real Amélie, would never be seen again.

There was so much to take in, so much to learn – but surely she knew so much already? After all, unlike the other agents, she'd already survived on the streets of Paris – she *knew* the streets of Paris.

"… six weeks, that's all. We like to be honest with our men and, um, women, it's the least we can do given what we're asking of you…"

"Six weeks…"

"Yes, six weeks is the life expectancy for our agents once they reach France."

Buckmaster stopped talking, took a sip from his cup of tea; he had a proper cup and saucer like in a smart hotel.

"So," he resumed, "it is at this point that I say to you: you do not have to go. You can return your papers, your suitcase, your clothes and we will return you to the Manor. You have skills we can use there. There is no disgrace in changing your mind, none at all."

He gestured at the door. "Vera will see you out, call you a cab, sort all that out, probably still treat you to a spot of lunch knowing Vera."

He tossed Vera a smile, then returned his attention to Amélie. She met his gaze.

"I want to go."

Buckmaster gave a nod. "I am sorry this all a bit of scramble – it's not how I like to work. I hate scrambling, but this is an emergency, we are in rather a pickle in Paris, you know the lie of the land and by all accounts are rather good at scrambling."

He opened the folder again and took out two photographs. He put them face down on the desk.

"This emergency was caused by these two men. We lost our entire Paris network…"

"Musée, the Musée network – Cécile? What news of Cécile…"

"No," said Buckmaster, shaking his head. "I'm not talking about the Musée, that was not one of ours. As far as we know that's long gone and its people with it. In war people disappear all the time. We cannot waste time looking for them. I know nothing of any Cecily, I doubt very much she is…"

"Cécile."

Buckmaster ignored her interruption. He flicked over the first photograph.

"Hugo Bleicher, sometimes known as Colonel Henri – make sure you commit this face to memory. He is a German agent, he infiltrated our network, Physician, and we lost every single one of them."

Amélie leaned forward to study the photo. It was blurred, a snatched shot. It would not be easy to recognise him from this. She sat back.

Buckmaster flicked over the second photo and Amélie leaned forward once more. It too was blurry but there was no mistaking the man looking over his shoulder towards the camera.

"Raymond!" she gasped, put her hand over her mouth and then felt foolish.

"Who?"

"Raymond… he ran the Musée, he's… it was him… the traitor."

"Hummm," said Buckmaster, scribbling a note in the

folder. "Interesting, we didn't have a name for him. We only know he's French and helps Bleicher – he's Bleicher's scout, sniffs out Resistance folk. What can you tell us about him?"

She sat back and began talking, finishing with her seeing him tumble from the train.

"Well, that explains the limp," said Buckmaster when she was done. "Not ideal, him knowing you but can't be helped given the tight spot we're in. We need you Miss Dreyfus. But any sign of this Raymond or Bleicher, any suspicions whatsoever, stop what you're doing and get out at once. If you have the chance tell André..."

"André?"

"Yes, André, codename Renard – fox. You'll meet him tonight – you're going out together. He's going to run the new network – you'll be his courier. A radio operator is there already. The mission is to rebuild the network and take the fight to the Germans. The war is about to change course and we must have people in place in Paris for when it does. We cannot afford for Renard and you to fail, Miss Chocolat. Any questions?"

Silence settled on the room. Question after question danced through her mind, but there was one that stayed put. What if Raymond saw her? If he saw her she was doomed, and so was their network.

"Haircut," she said. She needed to look different, at least at first glance.

"What?"

"I want to cut my hair short, to here…" she gestured at the base of her neck.

"I don't think now is the time…" began Buckmaster.

"Yes," interrupted Vera, "I see – we'll get that arranged."

"Righto," said Buckmaster. He gathered the two photographs and returned them to the folder. "Good, and good luck."

"Lunch time," said Vera and opened the door.

"Oh, one last thing Miss Dreyfus," said Buckmaster. Amélie paused in the doorway. "A will, have you made a will?"

Amélie shrugged. "What is a will?"

"Um," said Buckmaster. "It's, um, a document written by you setting out who gets your possessions should you… should you…"

"Be killed."

"Yes." He stared hard at her.

Amélie shrugged. "Why would I need a will – I have nothing."

Chapter 29

The constant whine of the small aeroplane's engine made conversation impossible. Amélie wriggled her toes, her feet were freezing. She could feel the cold on the back of her neck. Her hair was short now; a bob was what the hairdresser in the Ritz called it. "All the rage," he said. In the distance Amélie caught the thin white line of a searchlight, but it wasn't looking for them. Not yet.

Her stomach leapt as they hit another pocket of turbulence. The pilot stuck a thumb up. They were in a line in the cockpit, in front the pilot, a fresh-faced young man with sandy hair and a permanent smile, behind him André and then squeezed into the back Amélie. She had her suitcase on her lap as well as two guns, small machine guns, ice cold, bringers of death. She was to hand them over to their reception party, and couldn't wait to be rid of them.

The plane, a Lysander, or 'Land-anywhere' as the pilots called them, was heading for a field outside the city of Tours, south west of Paris, where they would be met by the local Resistance. They would be taken into the city and from there make their own way to Paris.

Amélie closed her eyes. She felt sick. Her Ritz lunch, a warm, sticky stew and potatoes followed by a large slice of cake with a dollop of ice cream (the largest meal she'd eaten since the war began), bounced around her tummy. She didn't like flying. She swallowed and her ears popped again. This would be the first and last time. She would never, ever, she vowed to herself, fly again – she would have been better off swimming home.

At least she was going home. She opened her eyes. André's head, clad like hers in a leather flying cap, rolled as they bounced down through the cloud line. They must be getting close.

Vera had introduced them at the airfield. She'd taken Amélie into an empty office where she supervised her getting changed into her French clothes, making one last check she'd nothing that might link her to Britain. When Amélie was dressed Vera made her go through every pocket.

"All it takes is one forgotten train ticket to Tunbridge Wells and that's it," she said. When they were done Vera reached into her handbag and took out a small box. "For you," she said. "I like to give all my girls a going-away present – this is yours."

Amélie opened the box, a silver necklace was curled neatly on white tissue. From it hung a crescent moon. "I couldn't get you a star could I," said Vera. "So I thought the moon was the next best thing."

She took it out of the box. "May I put it on?" she said. Amélie turned around. "Do you want me to take this one off?" Her mother's necklace and the apartment key had hung around her neck every day since she'd left home.

"Non," said Amélie. "I'll wear both." She felt Vera's hands tremble as she fixed the necklace in place.

"Come back safe."

Amélie turned around. "I won't come back – I'm going home remember."

Vera smiled. "Well, be safe then, my darling."

The door opened before Amélie could reply.

"Hello, hello, hello."

"You?" said Amélie.

"Me."

"You know each other?" said Vera.

"Yes… no…" said Amélie.

"She caught me in the bath, Aunty V."

224

"Oh for goodness sake," tutted Vera. "Clémentine, codename Chocolat, meet André, code name Renard."

"An old fox compared to you," said André. "School on holiday is it?"

Amélie put out her hand to shake his, but as he took hers, a lopsided grin flickering across his face, she flicked out her other hand, grasped him by the elbow and before he could say "What the blazes!" had spun him round and pinned him against the wall with his arm bent behind him. Just as the instructor at Arisaig had taught her.

"Ouch," he spluttered into the wall. "You win."

She let go and he turned to face her. "Point made, Clémentine."

He put his hand out and this time she shook it.

"If you two have quite finished," said Vera, "you have a plane to catch."

"Urgh," said Amélie as the plane lurched again. The pilot was gesturing to the left. She looked out of the cockpit and saw the broad silver squiggle of the Loire river. The plane dropped lower. The pilot had told them to look out for the signal from the ground when they saw the Loire.

She stared into the blackness below and wondered if she should feel scared. She put her hand to her neck and fiddled with her necklaces, grasped the key to home. What if the

Tours network had been taken over by the Germans and it was the Gestapo waiting for their arrival? Two Secret Service agents would be a prize catch. But she didn't feel scared. Not yet, she felt uncomfortable, and sick – she just wanted to get out of this plane. That was all. She swallowed and her ears popped.

"There," yelled André and bashed his finger against the cockpit window.

Below, although not far below so swiftly had the Lysander descended, a yellow light flared, then another. Soon there was a row of six small fires burning. The pilot flew over them and Amélie peered down. A dark figure stood and waved by each fire.

The pilot banked and turned for landing. "Oooffftt," said Amélie as they hit the ground hard, hopped into the air again, bounced a couple more times and came to a halt. Behind them the signal fires were already being extinguished.

Amélie pulled off her flying hat and replaced it with the beret she'd been given at the flat. She liked the way it looked with her new haircut. She angled it on her head like the young women did in Paris. She'd often imagined herself as one of them, tried to walk like them on the way back from school with Madeleine. Until one of them, usually Amélie, got the giggles.

The pilot turned off the engine and slid back the canopy. He peered over his shoulder.

"Good luck," he said as figures emerged from the night.

André clambered out on to the wing. He slid his suitcase down it and on to the grass, then took a crate from inside the aircraft and held it carefully.

"Welcome to France," said a Resistance fighter in accented English. He had a rifle strapped across his back and looked no older than Amélie. "I am Hugo."

"Take this," said André. "Easy with it, it's the explosives."

Hugo grinned. "Kaboom!" he said and took the crate.

Amélie handed the machine guns and her suitcase to André. She eased herself out of her seat and stepped on to the wing. Another fighter put his hand out. She took it and jumped down on to the grass.

"Home," she whispered.

An older man appeared. "Quick," he ordered. "Get the plane turned. We must get out of here."

Amélie took her and André's cases and moved them out the way. The Resistance fighters gathered by the Lysander's tail.

"Un, deux, trois…" said the older man and together they lifted and swung the plane around until it was facing back down the make-shift runway. The pilot gave the thumbs-up and slid the canopy shut.

"Stand back," said André and the noise of the propeller cut through the night.

Amélie looked around. "Don't worry," said Hugo, leaning close so his voice might be heard above the engine. "The Boche won't hear it above their fat snores."

They watched the Lysander bounce across the field and then, as if taken by a magic spell, lift up into the sky. Soon it was gone from sight and not long after the soft moan of the engine was gone too.

"Have you been to France before, Mademoiselle?" said Hugo, taking her case and leading her across the field as though he were a baggage boy making polite conversation in a smart hotel.

"Oui," said Amélie.

"Welcome back," said Hugo. He pointed at the horse and cart at the side of the field. The horse whinnied a hurry-up of its own. "Your carriage awaits."

Amélie took a deep breath. Time to become Clémentine.

Chapter 30

"You follow behind – not too close so if I am stopped…"

"Yes, yes," snapped Clémentine. "I have done this before."

"Sorry," said Hugo. His face fell.

"No, no" she said, "I'm sorry – I'm just tired."

"Can you ride…"

"A bicycle? Yes I can." Clémentine fastened her suitcase to the back of the bike.

"Your French is very good, Mademoiselle," said Hugo, one foot on the pedal of his bike.

She shot him a smile. She was tired and cold, but he was just doing his job. A brave boy.

"Could we go past the cathedral – it would help me to see it?"

"Of course," said Hugo, pushing his bike and swinging

himself on board. "But we must hurry if you are to catch your train."

It took an hour to cycle into Tours, to add to the freezing hour in the horse and cart getting them from the field in the middle of nowhere to a farmhouse where a large red-cheeked woman poured a bowl of piping hot soup down them. Clémentine had been allowed a rest – she would take a later train to André. He gave her the address of a safe house near the Gare Montparnasse in Paris where they would meet later.

It was light by the time they reached Tours. On the edge of the city, where the road ran alongside a pavement that in turn followed the Loire's gentle curve, a checkpoint had been set up. A barricade was lowered across the road, manned by four gendarmes and four German soldiers. The soldiers sat sleepily in the back of a truck leaving the policemen to check the small queue of farm vehicles on the way to market.

Hugo stopped to allow her to catch up. "They're not interested in cyclists. They're after smugglers. Stay close this time, stop if they say stop. It'll be fine, you have your papers."

"Are you sure?" said Clémentine. She was breathing quickly… all it took was a glimpse of those grey uniforms again.

"There is no other way," said Hugo. "Come, or we'll attract attention."

He pedalled off, taking the pavement rather than the road. She took a deep breath and followed. "Paulie and Maman and Papa," she hummed to herself. "Paulie and Maman and Papa…"

Out of the corner of her eye she watched the soldiers. They paid the two cyclists no attention. One gendarme looked up from his check of a farmer's papers. His eyes followed them for a moment, but only a moment.

By the time they stopped outside the cathedral 20 minutes later, Clémentine's heart had sunk from her mouth to its more usual position.

"It's beautiful isn't it," said Hugo, waving an arm at the cathedral.

She nodded. She wanted to be on the train, be in Paris, back where she knew the streets.

"And I'll tell you something else for nothing," continued Hugo. On the surface he seemed to be fearless but Clémentine knew underneath it would be different. "Round the corner on Rue Colbert, number 39, that's where the Maid of Orleans had her armour made."

"Joan of Arc?"

"Yes – I think of her sometimes. We need to be strong

231

like her, brave. I bet you're like the Maid, I can tell – I have a sense like that. That's what the others say…"

His words trailed off, as though he felt he'd made himself look foolish.

Clémentine smiled at him. "Thank you," she said. "I will try to be like her."

She thought of the Maid several hours later. A check of her papers on the train as they approached Paris, a man in a leather coat, Gestapo probably.

She told him of the splendid cathedral in Tours that took her breath away, and did he know round the corner was where Joan of Arc had her armour made for her fight against the terrible English. He smiled at that, returned her papers and didn't order her to open her suitcase.

"Thank you, Hugo," said Clémentine to herself.

Half an hour later she stepped onto the platform at Gare Montparnasse and walked business-like towards the nearest exit – never loiter in a station, always look like you know where you are going.

She descended the stairs to the Metro, travelled four stops, got off, changed platforms and at the last moment boarded a train heading back the way she'd come. Two stops later she got off and hurried up the stairs. Outside the station she crossed the road and pretended to study the dresses in a shop window while she watched in the glass for a breathless man to emerge from the station trying to keep up with her.

None did. She wasn't being followed.

Paris was the same, smelt the same, looked the same, but it was different. The colour had gone from the city, as if the Germans had taken that as well as the food, the cars – and as many Jewish people as they could find.

Clémentine walked for a time before heading for the safe house – just to make doubly sure nobody was tailing her – and she noticed another change. The Germans had installed their own street signs. Pinned over the French ones were directions in long German words that meant nothing to her. But she knew her way. This was her city and nobody was going to take it from her.

A soldier, in a soft cap rather than a helmet which meant he was off duty, cycled past her whistling happily. He stopped outside a café and leant his bike against the wall. She watched him go in, saw him seated towards the rear, his back to the window, and without breaking stride took the bike and wheeled it around the nearest corner. She looked about, nobody had seen her. She hooked her suitcase on the handlebars, climbed onto the bike and pedalled it away, making for the safe house. Halfway there she leant the bike against a wall, took her suitcase and walked on.

An old woman answered the door, opening it a crack. Clémentine gave the code word. The woman nodded opened the door fully and pointed upstairs. André smiled when she walked into the room. It felt reassuring to see him again. He was sitting at a table with another man.

"This is Gilbert, our radio operator."

They shook hands. Gilbert was small and serious looking with a pale, pinched face.

"You will be the go-between for me and Gilbert."

Clémentine nodded.

"Good," said André. "Well then, shall we get started?"

Chapter 31

Gilbert was a man of few words, as if he didn't have time for talking. Which suited Clémentine just fine. There was no time for friendships and no desire on Clémentine's part. She didn't need anyone. That's what she told herself when she lay in bed at night, shivering in whichever apartment was her home for a few nights. She would have everyone she wanted when Maman and Papa and Paulie came home after the war.

André was more chatty, and she couldn't help liking him despite trying not to care. He liked to joke about the food, which by the winter of 1943 was even worse than the school meals in England. Meat, eggs, butter and cheese were rarely seen – when they were Clémentine would lay their happy meal on the table and they would stare at it for an age before eating, devouring it first with their eyes, doubly satisfied.

The Germans had food, and so did any who helped them – and there were plenty of those in Paris; betrayal was always around the next corner. For the rest it was an endless diet of macaroni and mashed turnip, macaroni and grated turnip, macaroni and brussel sprouts, grated or mashed.

In the countryside children hunted hedgehogs, grass snakes, frogs, squirrels, anything to add to the pot. In Paris the mayor felt it necessary to issue a warning over the dangers of eating stewed cat. Family cats across the city breathed a sigh of relief.

Queues for the shops were longer than ever. Cycling through the streets in the pre-dawn darkness, Clémentine watched hopeful women line up outside the bakers and butchers. Children were given special milk rations but she was not supposed to be a child anymore.

She didn't know what she was. She was still hiding, still good at hiding. But the girl who hid in the cupboard was gone.

She and André would play a game of their own when getting ready for a mission, taking it in turns to select the meal they would have when the war was over. André chose what he called Sunday dinner with roast beef and all the trimmings, which sounded suspiciously British and brown. She went for her father's version of Coq au Vin, served at home in their kitchen, the steam from the cooking fugging up the windows, her Maman cackling as she sat at the kitchen table, drinking wine that was supposed to go in the dinner and sharing the day's gossip. Afterwards they would leave the washing-up piled in the sink and go out for crepes, warm, chocolate crepes dusted with icing sugar...

"Enough," said André, rolling his eyes. "I can't take any more."

Most of the missions were simple; taking André's messages to Gilbert to be radioed back to London. Clémentine would roll them up and push them into the handlebars of her bike, or fold them in newspapers and leave them in the bike's basket because they were easy to get rid of if necessary.

Cold and hungry and often scared, they survived the winter. Slowly, and carefully, André rebuilt the network. Sometimes he would have Clémentine sit in on a meeting with a new recruit in a café or on a park bench and once they were gone ask her opinion.

Trust no-one, trust no-one, trust no-one.

It whispered through Clémentine's mind as she studied the recruits, watched their lips move, trying to see if the words coming out were lies. And all the time she kept an eye out for Raymond. She wanted to see him, wanted to tell André and set a trap for the traitor.

While Gilbert was on the radio to London she would wait outside, hunched in her coat, feeling the cold take her toes then sneak up her legs, looking out for the German radio detection vans that crawled through the streets hunting prey.

She would think about trapping Raymond, getting revenge because it made her feel better than thinking about Cécile, worrying what had become of her, missing her and, above all, worrying about Maman, Papa and Paulie and missing them so much it ached.

A van with distinctive wires on its roof, like two connected coat hangers, had turned into the street, its engine purring gently as it edged towards her, the coat hangers rotating one way then the other, searching for radio signals. It stopped.

Her heart raced. A car rolled to a halt behind it. There were bulky figures inside. The hangers were still rotating which meant they were not absolutely sure yet where the signal was coming from – but they were close.

She pulled the door open a crack and slipped into the apartment block's communal hall. There was no lock on the door. Two bikes poked out from beneath the stairs. She pulled one out and laid it on the floor just inside the door – it wouldn't stop anyone but it might trip and delay a Gestapo officer in a hurry.

Clémentine raced up the stairs, taking them two at a time. The temptation to bang on Gilbert's door and scream a warning itched through her. Instead, when she reached the third floor she took a breath and rapped out the agreed signal.

Gilbert looked angry when he opened the door.

"Boche," hissed Clémentine. "Outside."

He left the door open and ran for the bedroom where the radio was set up. She shut the door and followed him in. He was scrabbling with the aerial, pulling it down.

"The papers…" He waved at the small pile on the small desk next to the transmitter. "Get rid of them."

She gathered them and rushed into the kitchen. At the far end was a large fireplace, big enough for someone to stand in – the block once housed larger, grand apartments before being divided up. There was no fire lit. What could she do with the papers?

She heard herself groan. Hurried footsteps on the stairs, heavy boots. A second of silence. Her eyes flew around the room. Gilbert appeared in the doorway to the bedroom. He had a revolver in his hand. A fist pounded on the door to the apartment.

"Hide," he hissed.

Hide, she thought. Hide… where. A story flashed into

her mind, one her mother read her, The Scarlet Pimpernel, an English spy who rescued French aristocrats, saving them from the guillotine, one adventure, an escape up a chimney. It's how chimneys are built in grand houses, with rungs for sweeps to climb. She ducked and stepped into the fireplace.

It was dark. She reached out her hand, running it up the chimney shaft, higher and higher, on her tiptoes... her fingers felt something metal. She wrapped her fingers around it, a rung, she let it take her weight and it held.

Another banging on the door, this time accompanied by a shouted threat.

"Open or we shoot the door down."

"Coming," she heard Gilbert say.

She stuffed the papers into the band of her skirt and flung her other hand up, her feet scrabbling against the soot-covered bricks of the chimney.

BANG!

The shot rang out loud and Clémentine screamed. Another shot drowned the sound of her horror. Gilbert had aimed at the door and fired. There was a yell from outside followed by the splintering of wood as the Germans kicked the door down, another deafening crack from Gilbert's revolver this time answered by the rapid rattle of a machine gun.

Clémentine pulled with every grain of strength and lifted herself up into the chimney. She reached out again and found another rung, and another. She climbed into the darkness. Below came another angry stutter of machine gun fire, the crash of a table and chairs being knocked over, shouts in German, boots thundering down to the kitchen. More shouts. Clémentine froze.

Barked orders echoed up the chimney. She closed her eyes. More sounds rose to her. They were smashing up the apartment, searching for secrets. Searching for her? There was nothing to say she'd been here. Her nose tickled. The soot was sneaking up it. She wanted to sneeze. Her arms ached.

It was the size of the apartment that saved her. It did not take the Germans long to search it. They took Gilbert with them. Dead or alive, Clémentine had no idea.

She hung on for another few minutes, just to be sure then clambered down into the kitchen. Or what had once been the kitchen. The cupboards had been ripped apart, the floorboards smashed to pieces. Everything was wrecked. Apart from the mirror that hung next to the front door — always next to the front door, the people of Paris liked to check on themselves before they left home.

A soot-smeared face stared back at Clémentine. Her

clothes too were dyed dark. She looked like a chimney sweep from one of her story books.

She bent over the sink in the kitchen and splashed water on her face. She must warn André. There was a pool of blood on the floor by what was left of the front door. She stepped over it and hurried down the stairs.

They would have left someone to watch the apartment, but, Clémentine gambled, they would be on the lookout for people arriving, not leaving. It was fewer than 20 steps she reckoned to the corner, where her bike lent against the wall. Once on that nobody would catch her. She took a breath and opened the door to the building. She didn't look round, kept her head down and walked. One, two, three, four, five, six, seven, eight, nine... halfway.

She could feel eyes boring into her back. Her shoulders tensed, waiting for an order to stop. Sixteen, seventeen... she ran. She couldn't help it.

"HALT!"

She was round the corner, into the alleyway. There was her bike, still propped in the alcove. In a flash she was on it, a hasty push and she was away.

Chapter 32

Anew radio operator arrived with spring. She was called Claudette and spoke French just as you'd imagine a young Englishwoman might speak French. But she was fluent in Morse Code, the fastest Clémentine had seen and that mattered most.

Gilbert's fate was unknown and there was no time to dwell on him either. He was pushed into a locked room in Clémentine's mind. Close the door, turn the key and get on with trying to make it to tomorrow.

The weather improved, the trees blossomed, green shoots were sighted and it was impossible not to believe in a brighter future.

There was hope in the Parisian air in the spring of 1944. Clémentine could smell it as she cycled around the city. Whisper it quietly, but the talk was this year would, at long last, bring the invasion and, perhaps – perhaps, even liberation.

Clémentine didn't dare let herself think about that. Because, and this was a thought that hung over her on sleepless nights, if it was over she would find out if Maman, Papa and Paulie were coming home. Or if they were…

Clémentine shook her head. She was climbing the steps from the Metro, a newspaper in her basket, in which was folded the next message for Claudette to send back to London, alongside a small bunch of carrots she'd been delighted to discover at the market. Just a little thing but enough to put a spring in her step. It was a warm day. Hope in the air, but danger still lurked around every corner.

Outside the station a checkpoint had been set up. There were men in leather jackets inside the entrance looking out for anyone who turned back. She had no choice but to join the queue.

She felt sweat prickle her back. A warm day, but not that warm. It didn't matter how many times she faced danger it never became any easier.

She shuffled forward a few steps. Someone was pushing behind, impatient to get on.

"Hey," the woman in front of her turned round and protested. She smiled at Clémentine.

"Not you, luvvie – them at the back… why they in such a hurry to get sniffed…"

She let out a little laugh, pleased with what she'd said.

"Sniffed?" said Clémentine. "You mean searched?"

"Non, non," said the woman, "they've got one of those physionomistes here. Read in the papers about them but never seen one before. Good job I had a wash this morning as we're gonna be inspected, eh?"

She guffawed at her joke and nudged Clémentine.

"A physio-what?"

"Nomiste – a physionomiste, you know one of these men who says they can tell a Jew by their smell, or is it their look? Can never remember… no, yes, their look that's it. Was in the papers – the Jews look a particular way, that's what they say."

"That sounds stupid," said Clémentine, eyes darting here and there, "besides haven't they all been taken?"

The woman shrugged. "They are masters of deception – difficult to get rid of, tricky sorts… but this man will spot 'em. You'll see, it's the looks he can tell. He'll spot 'em. We're well rid of 'em if you ask me."

Clémentine opened her mouth. And closed it again. The woman was around the same age as her mother, probably a mother also. How could she say such things? How could she think such things?

The queue shuffled forward. At the front two soldiers held two guard dogs, two Gendarmes brought people forward two at a time, checked their papers then stood them in front of three men in ankle length leather coats. The one in the middle, hatless – and hairless too, a strange looking man with a long pointy nose and pointy ears that made him resemble a goblin – lent forward and stared into their faces. He seemed to stare for an age then leaned forward as if to greet them in the French manner, with a kiss on either cheek, but instead turned each of their heads so he could look at them in profile. He tapped his finger against his pursed lips.

Clémentine swallowed. The sweat on her back felt cold and she shivered.

"You all right, dear," said the woman. "Look like you've seen a ghost."

"Um, yes, fine... it's just I'm going to be late for..."

"Aren't we all, dear, aren't we all."

Clémentine glanced back towards the station. This couldn't be real.

"Next," called the gendarmes and an old man and woman shuffled forward holding hands.

Could it?

"There's no way out, my dear," said the woman.

"No, I just wonder whether I should bother – I'll miss my appointment so I might as well get the Metro back home…"

"Next."

Two women directly in front of them were beckoned towards the men in leather coats.

"Nearly there now," said the woman and slipped her arm through Clémentine's. "Won't take a minute… unless you've something to hide, my dear."

Clémentine caught the sideways glance the woman gave her. She tried to make herself smile.

One of the gendarmes put his arm out and gestured for them.

"You two," he said. "Quick, quick, we've not got all day. Papers…"

Clémentine switched her basket to her left hand – the newspaper poked out invitingly – and dug in her pocket for her papers.

The woman had already handed hers over.

"There," said the gendarme and pointed at the men in leather coats.

The woman resumed her firm grip on Clémentine's arm and stepped forward.

"My papers," said Clémentine, reaching her hand out to take them back.

"We see the physionomiste first, don't we officer," said the woman, tugging Clémentine in front of the leather coats.

Clémentine stared at the ground, eyes fixed on a broken cobble near the physionomiste's right boot.

"Look up," he snapped and Clémentine, startled, lifted her head. His eyes were hypnotic, they drew hers in, she felt her head beginning to spin. He leaned forward, studying her close enough for Clémentine to hear the snort of him breathing in. He stepped back and, in a movement so swift Clémentine saw only a blur, lifted his right hand and clicked his fingers.

"Her," he barked.

The other two leather coats, who'd been leaning on the barrier post, jerked upright, as if surprised by his sudden selection. One of the dogs was startled too and pulled against its leash, leaning forward and barking at Clémentine and the woman.

"Take her," said the physionomiste and Clémentine felt the blood drain to her toes. Her head spun.

"No," she said, her voice little more than a whisper. She thought she might faint.

"Are you all right, Mademoiselle?" said the physionomiste.

He put a hand on her arm, concern on his smooth face. "This can happen when you're so close to one of them."

Clémentine pulled away, disgusted by his touch. She wanted to be sick, her mouth dropped open. The woman was being hustled towards a van by the two leather coats.

"No," the woman said, looking back over her shoulder. "Nooo," she repeated, this time louder and longer. "I don't look anything like 'em. This is a mistake, my husband he's a gendarme, he'll tell you... we hate 'em... we hate 'em..."

Her voice was cut off by the slamming of the van doors.

Clémentine swallowed. She dragged her gaze back to the physionomiste.

"Run along now, Mademoiselle," he said. "I'm sure you've somewhere you should be."

The gendarme handed her papers back. He gestured for her to move on and swung his attention back to the queue.

"Next," he barked.

Chapter 33

There were good days. Or rather good nights. There was the night she acted as look out for André and his sabotage team when they clambered over a factory wall and planted a bomb in the building where engines for German tanks were made.

She counted them all back over the wall shut them up in the smelly butcher's van André had borrowed, watched them drive away and then waited, left behind to make sure the bomb went off. Thirty-minute fuses, André had said. She got her bike ready, checked her watch. When she estimated there were three minutes to go she set off, bouncing over the cobbles, her coat flapping in the breeze.

She ducked when the bomb went off, a thwwwup followed by a violin crescendo of breaking glass, and kept pedalling and, just for good measure, let out a whoop of joy.

Another night she dived into a canal to replace a fuse that had come loose from the bomb fixed to a lock gate. The men stood umming and ahhing to disguise what was obvious to Clémentine – none of them would get in the water. She stripped to her vest and pants and dived in. It was dark and cold, but being in water never bothered her. She took a breath and pulled herself down the lock door by its wooden slats, found the bomb, came back up for another breath and the fuse, went down again and fixed it in place.

André gave her his jersey to dry herself and then his coat to put on over hers as she shivered in the van on the way back to Paris. The bomb went off, destroyed the lock and interrupted the flow of barges carrying petrol for German tanks.

There was more to do, always more to do. Something was happening. Something was coming. The Invasion? Were the Americans and British really going to cross the Channel and set France free?

The Germans hit back. Arrests increased. People were rounded up in the street. Men were sent to Germany to work in factories. Women's papers were checked and double checked – just a whiff of suspicion and it was off to the Gestapo cells beneath the Avenue Foch. They said you could hear the screams from out on the Avenue. Nobody walked down the Avenue Foch anymore.

There were checks everywhere. Fear walked the streets, crouched in the corner of every home – it was there each morning when Clémentine opened her eyes. Paris clung on, hanging on to the hope that help was on the way. One day... one day soon?

With each arrest, each Resistance fighter they lost – and they were losing more and more – her heart hardened. She had work to do. She wasn't Amélie, she was Clémentine.

She stared at the mirror in her bedroom. She was staying with an old woman, in her tiny spare room. She looked at herself and wondered when it would end. She felt tired.

"Who am I?" she whispered the question.

She paused as if waiting for an answer. She knew she had to be someone else for the war, needed to be Clémentine if she wanted to survive, and then after the war she could go back to who she was.

"What," she asked herself out loud, "if I like another me better?"

She dressed swiftly, banishing her thoughts as she angled her green beret on her head – it was her favourite thing. She smiled at herself in the mirror.

"Bonjour, Clémentine."

The old woman, the block's concierge which made it easy for Clémentine to come and go, leaned on her brush and directed a rare smile at her when she stepped outside. The woman beckoned Clémentine over with a nod of her head.

"It's come," she said, her voice little louder than a whisper.

"Pardon?" said Clémentine, thinking of her rendezvous. She didn't have time to waste.

The woman dropped her voice even lower. "The invasion," she said and her eyes widened in delight as she spoke.

Clémentine felt her heart leap. The woman gripped her arm. "They are coming… they are coming."

On her ride to the cemetery Clémentine saw people smiling, and she smiled too. It would still be a while before the Americans reached Paris but they would – one day not too far away. Until then… the Germans were still here.

She leaned her bike against the wall by the back entrance to the Père-Lachaise Cemetery. She was to meet her contact at the grave of Jean-Batiste Pezon, the famous lion tamer. His gravestone was a statue of him riding his pet lion, the lion that one day decided it'd had enough of being ridden around a circus ring and ate him. Clémentine sometimes wondered what happened to the lion.

Her contact, who she met here every Tuesday morning, ran one of their safe houses. She didn't know its address, didn't know anything about him beyond the name he used, Gérard. It never lasted more than five minutes. She gave him instructions from André, he voiced any concerns or problems.

"Oh, one more thing – there's a man who wants to meet you," said Gérard, his eyes shifting up and down the cemetery path, always on the lookout.

"Who?"

Trust no-one. Trust no-one. Trust no-one.

"Calls himself Marc, says he knows of you, knows you're working for the network, says he can help us, has a network of his own – wants to join forces."

"How?"

Gérard shrugged.

"What d'you think?"

Gérard shrugged again. "Dunno… be careful."

Clémentine nodded. "Where?"

He gave her the address and time.

Trust no-one. Trust no-one. Trust no-one.

She whistled to herself as she cycled to the address. This Marc would be there for an hour from midday on Tuesdays and Thursdays. She had time to get to there and find a place to watch any comings and goings well before midday.

She was on her second chestnut coffee – she couldn't stand the stuff, didn't know how adults could like it. She'd learnt a lot about pretending over the last couple of years. She took a sip, grimaced and over the rim of the cup saw him approach the apartment building.

She let out a little sigh. She'd known it would be him, one of those gut instincts and gut instincts can keep you alive. Apart from the limp, he didn't look to have changed; the war had not worn him down like everyone else.

"Hello, Raymond," she said softly as he stopped in the doorway to the apartment and looked around. His eyes passed over the café, over the girl in the green beret sitting at one of the outside tables beneath the red awning, but didn't stop.

She waited until he went in, slid a couple of coins on to the table, pushed her cup away but then changed her mind and emptied it with a gulp. Papa insisted they always finish a meal. "We are the fortunate," he would say every time as Paulie rolled his eyes at her across the table, "so let us clear our plates."

She kept her head bowed as she mounted her bike – just

in case he was looking out a window – and pedalled off to warn André they had a problem.

"Hummmm," said André.

He'd been in a good mood when she arrived.

"Ah, Clémentine," he said. "Thought you might be the Americans hot foot from the beaches of Normandy."

"Normandy?"

"Yes, that's where they landed this morning – took the Boche by surprise. Still a long way from Paris but they are on the way."

"How long?"

"Two months… three maybe, perhaps longer." He saw the disappointment on her face. She'd become good at not allowing her emotions to show. But this… the beginning of the end had got to her, made her hope. Weeks she'd thought, weeks and she'd be home and Maman would be home and Paulie and Papa.

"They will come, Clémentine, they will come."

She smiled at André. She'd come to regard him as a brother. Almost. A pretend big brother. Which was why she didn't want to tell him about Raymond – who wants to be the bearer of bad news? But she had to.

"We have to get rid of him – and fast."

André paced up and down the room, the dining room of

a large apartment with views over the River Seine. A friendly Count had lent it to the Resistance for "as long as there is a German boot in my beautiful Paris".

"You have to use me – I have to be the bait," Clémentine said and sat down at the head of the table. "It's the only way."

André stopped at the far end of the table. He took a seat, facing her. "How on earth do they pass the salt?" His face straightened, became serious. He sighed. "Yes," he said. "You are right as always Clémentine."

He stood up again and paced towards her. "It's damn risky though…" He pulled out the chair on her right-hand side. "And after… I think this will be your last… well, all being well your last…"

"Non," snapped Clémentine. She couldn't imagine stopping. What would she do? She couldn't bear just to wait.

André held his hand up. "Even if we succeed in getting rid of him we can't risk you being seen – if he's told them about you others will be looking, Bleicher even. And if they catch you…"

"I'm not scared of that," said Clémentine, even though she knew she was.

"I know – I'm not sure you're scared of anything

Clémentine. But it's not just you I have to worry about. They take you and the whole network's at risk."

He stood up, walked behind her and put a gentle hand on her shoulder. "This will be your final mission."

Chapter 34

Clémentine stared up at the twin towers of Notre-Dame. In one of them were the bells, loud and heavy with history when they rang out across the city, 10 of them if she remembered correctly. They'd been taught at school, each had a name they were supposed to learn by heart. What were they called again? Denis, perhaps. Was that one?

She shook her head. It was a warm afternoon, one of those late spring days when it's impossible not to turn your face to the sun and let your mind drift away. She felt hot with her beret on, wondered if she was going red in the face. She hated it when she went red. Paulie had teased her once that she looked like someone had drawn a face on a tomato, which made her go even redder.

She needed the beret. She didn't want to run the risk

of Raymond spotting her until it was time. The arranged meeting place was inside the cathedral.

It was André's plan, most of it. They had to meet somewhere public so Raymond wouldn't be worried about anything happening to him. And busy, which would also reassure Raymond and help their plan. Bait the trap with Clémentine.

A crocodile of neat schoolchildren was ushered up the steps by a nun and into the cathedral two by two.

Clémentine ran her eye over the people outside the cathedral. There was a smattering of grey, German soldiers, off duty, seeing the sights. She scowled at a group of them who strolled past laughing at their day in the sun.

A car stopped on the edge of the square and a man climbed out of the back seat. He bent down to the front window to speak to the driver, patted the roof of the car and set off across the square. Clémentine watched the car – no-one else got out – then watched Raymond's limping progress towards the cathedral. She followed at a distance. He had one hand in his pocket and didn't look back.

Her eyes darted this way and that. There was no sign of any Gestapo shadowing Raymond. André was sure he would come alone. The Gestapo wouldn't be satisfied with Clémentine alone – they would want André and Claudette, the whole network. They always wanted more so they wouldn't rush. It would be Raymond's job to weasel his way into André's confidence and then the Gestapo would strike.

She knew how they worked, she knew he would try to convince her he was no traitor, perhaps even claim he was a double agent. He would tell her she didn't understand – she was just a girl, she had to take him to her boss, leave the men to work this out because they better understood the ways of war.

Inside the cathedral she took off her beret and dropped further behind Raymond. She blinked her eyes to accustom them to the dull light after the sunshine outside. She watched Raymond head down the nave, his head turning left and right.

She quickened her step until she was behind him. She swallowed. She could reach out and touch him, touch the traitor, the man who'd condemned Cécile. This is what André had worried about – she would let anger cloud her judgement. But he needn't have worried. She knew exactly what she had to do.

She put out a hand and touched his shoulder. He spun round.

"Follow me," she said, avoiding his eyes.

"Vette," he said. He recognised her at once, despite

her haircut. A smile curved over his face. He looked like a hungry wolf. "My little Vette."

For a moment Clémentine was lost. Vette? Who was Vette? She looked up at him. She'd remembered clever eyes. But they weren't.

"Follow me," she repeated.

She led him to the south door and back into the sunshine. She pushed her beret into her pocket. For some reason she didn't want him to see it.

"Where are we going?" he said, walking down the steps beside her.

She ignored him and flicked her gaze back and forth. She was in control. Use his surprise to get him moving, before he can think – so André had instructed her.

"Follow me."

They turned left into the tree-lined gardens next to the cathedral. Over the wall the river was full and in a rush, the spring waters hurrying through Paris and all the way to the Channel, the seaside, the beaches where Maman rolled up her bloomers and paddled shrieking with mock-horror at the cold.

"You're taking me to meet your new boss?"

Clémentine glanced round at him. "Yes," she said and saw his smile flicker again.

"I'm not who you think I am – you know that? You don't know what happened, you wouldn't understand. I can help your network, I have good contacts, we are a big group – are you with the British? Is this a British network?"

"He'll tell you all."

They crossed the Pont de Saint Louis to the neighbouring island, leaving the crowds behind. She didn't like this bridge. Everybody said it would be rebuilt properly once the Germans went. It was like walking into a cage. She glanced round at Raymond again. He seemed unconcerned.

On the far side she turned left and led him down stone steps to the walkway running along the river. Here, squeezed between the two islands, the river swirled, angry at its flow being interrupted.

A handful of chestnut trees, leaves shining green, marked the tip of the Île Saint-Louis. A bench sat beneath them. Two men had erected easels and were painting the view of the river, Notre-Dame rising above it.

"Sit on the bench," said Clémentine.

Raymond glanced around and did as instructed.

"Stay there," she said. "He will join you."

She looked up towards the street. All quiet. Back along the walkway. All quiet.

"Okay," she said.

The two men put down their paintbrushes. Clémentine walked past them.

"Keep watch," said one, his hand digging into his pocket.

"Are you the boss?" Clémentine heard Raymond say as she turned the corner on the walkway so she could keep an eye on the steps.

She'd never been down here before, looking up at her city, the sun beginning to set and bathing it in a golden light. She loved Paris. She never wanted to leave. She wanted this to end.

"Non," she said and spun on her heel. When she turned the corner she saw Raymond kneeling on the riverbank, one of André's men standing behind him pointing a pistol.

"Non," she said louder and the three of them looked round. She put out her hand. "I'll do this," she said.

"But…" said André's man.

"This is my operation – I'm in charge. That's what André said. You two, keep watch."

The man shrugged, nodded at his companion, and placed the pistol in her right hand. It felt cold.

She watched them until they were out of sight around the corner.

"Vette?" said Raymond. He kept his head bowed but tilted it a little towards her. "I'm not what they think…"

His voice wobbled.

"Stand up and turn around," ordered Clémentine. She knew, she absolutely knew, what she should do. She closed her eyes for a moment and saw Cécile, saw Cécile smiling at her, the bravery and goodness shining out of her.

Raymond took a step towards her. She raised the pistol.

"No," he said and put his hands out as if they might stop the bullet.

"Jump," said Clémentine.

"What?"

"In the river – jump, get out into the stream or I will shoot you."

"Wait… but…"

"I'll count to three."

"Vette…"

"Un…"

He took a step backwards, still facing her.

"Deux."

She wrapped her finger around the trigger. Raymond turned, glanced back over his shoulder.

"Trois…"

He leapt as she fired. The bullet pinged into the river, where it had been aimed, well away from him. It barely made a mark on the surface. The splash made by the startled

Raymond did, but not for long. His head emerged from the grey water, his arms floundering as he tried to keep himself afloat. He spat a mouthful of water.

"Urgh," said Clémentine. "Imagine having to drink from the Seine."

She raised her voice so he could hear. "It's where you belong, rat."

"I'll… I'll…" began Raymond, the current beginning to take him away from her, "kill you Vette…" He swallowed another mouthful of water and by the time he'd spat that out the river had him and was dragging him away. She never heard the rest of his threats.

"So long, Raymond," said Amélie as the two Resistance men arrived at her side. They stared at the figure disappearing down river, splashing out in an attempt to head for the far bank.

"Should've killed him," mumbled one.

"No," said Clémentine.

He would get out – at least he should – but not there. The current would see to that, whisk him downriver, give them plenty of time to get away. They'd shut down Gérard's safe-house; there would be no trace for Raymond or the Gestapo to follow. No loose ends.

Chapter 35

André was insistent. Her time as a courier was over. And so, Amélie insisted, it meant her time as Clémentine should end too. André objected. This went against the way things were done.

"But that's what we were taught – not to do things the way they are done," said Amélie. "I want to be me again."

André looked up from the kitchen table. He was chopping a carrot and parsnip with the same care he encoded messages for Claudette to send to London. They were making soup, or stew, or perhaps something in between. Mush, Amélie preferred to call it.

The windows in the apartment were open. Summer was here. The Allies still weren't. "Soon," everyone assured each other raising voices above rumbling stomachs. "Soon…

soon… soon…" Promises rose into the sunny skies, but hot air doesn't fill stomachs.

Paris was growing desperate. The closer the Allies came, the tighter the Germans gripped. Still Jews were sought and found, Resistance groups broken up and their broken members packed on to trains heading east. And when the trains came back they were empty. Nobody came back from the east.

Stories did, more and more of them, horror stories. Amélie heard them, mulled them over for a time, then locked them away with all the rest of the dark matter and longed for it to end. For everything to be normal once more.

That's why she wanted to start being Amélie again. Not Clémentine. Or Chocolat. Or Vette. Or June. Just Amélie. She still looked over her shoulder, still looked for a way out everywhere she went, spotting dark alleys, hiding places, back doors, open windows. She would always do that. Forever and ever.

André agreed. She could be Amélie again. She still worked for him and the network. Helping code messages and decode the ones received from London. She made mush and waited while André and his men went out to gather information, cut telephone wires, block train lines or blow up bridges and pylons.

She was confined to the apartment, not allowed out apart from doing the shopping, dull hours in long queues, or maybe a turn around the nearest park.

There was no sign of Raymond. He'd vanished. Amélie liked to think he'd taken his second chance and run away. She'd given him that chance so maybe, she hoped, pressing her eyes shut in bed, her good deed would see one in return for her. A return home for her family.

She'd begun dreaming of them again. For the first time since she'd left France for Britain. Maman and Papa stopped running from her in her dreams. She couldn't make out their faces because they looked the other way but with every dream she got a little closer. Maybe that was a sign. She prayed it might be.

"Don't you think," said André, sliding the carrot off the chopping board into the pot, "we should let someone else have a go at making the stew? Someone who might, well, make it a little less mushy?"

Amélie scowled at him. He grinned back. "What I mean to say is I have a job for you."

There was to be a protest in the streets, a Hunger March, on the first day of July. Amélie was to mix with the marchers, hand out leaflets telling people to get ready to fight, it was nearly time to rid their city of the invader.

So she put on her green beret angled from right to left on her head, beneath it a pair of sunglasses. Claudette lent her a summer dress, polka dots, and made her twirl before she left. She stuffed the leaflets in her satchel and walked to where the march was to begin.

When she stepped out of a side street on to the Rue du Faubourg-Saint-Denis her mouth dropped open. A throng of women – it was all women – were marching towards her. There were banners and chanting, voices raised together. "We want bread… we want bread… we want bread…"

She spotted the men in leather coats at once – there were plenty of them, skulking along the pavements but that didn't stop her spirits rising. As the marchers drew level she stepped into their ranks, raised her fist and started chanting too.

"We want bread… we want bread…

She took off her beret and her glasses – she didn't want to hide among these brave women. Smiling all the time she began to hand out leaflets. The women smiled back. It felt like they were together. At last, the women of Paris were together and leading the way to freedom.

The march reached the Place de la République. A line of trucks was drawn up on the far side outside the army barracks, some had machine guns mounted on them, pointing at the marchers, others were full of soldiers, sweating beneath their heavy helmets.

The march hesitated. Amélie watched a young woman, not much older than her, step forward and raise her fist. "Courage," she yelled. "We march."

She walked on into the square. "Courage," yelled Amélie as others took up the cry and they all stepped forward. Across the square the Germans watched, but did nothing.

The festive atmosphere returned and after more songs were sung and chants chanted, people began to drift away, jobs to do, hungry mouths to feed. Amélie felt a sadness take hold, her stomach rumbled. She felt hot and sweaty. She glanced in her satchel, only a few leaflets left. Time to go home.

A hand touched her shoulder. "Ohh," she said, spinning round expecting to see a leather coat.

"Pardon," said the woman. She had grey hair, swept back from her forehead into a tight plait. Her face was thin and worn, like the faces of so many women in Paris in 1944. "I didn't mean to…"

Amélie flashed a false smile and began to edge away. Something was not right.

"Wait," said the woman, raising a hand. "Are you…"

Amélie shook her head. She couldn't run, not yet. Running would attract the attention of the leather coats.

"Amélie…" said the woman.

Amélie, instinctively, took a step towards her.

"What?" She glanced behind her. What was going on? A trap? Raymond?

"Amélie… Amélie Dreyfus – it is you…"

"I think you've made a mistake," said Amélie. She fastened the buckle on her satchel. "Au revoir, Madame." She turned and began to walk, she needed to get out of the square.

"No, please… Amélie… your mother…"

Amélie froze. The women caught up with her, placed a hand on her arm, a gentle hand. "I was, I mean I am… a friend, I know her, I know your Maman."

Chapter 36

"I thought it was you… I haven't seen you since, well, since before all this. You look like your brother, you know, with your hair cut short. Just like your brother…"

Madame Strauss fell silent. Amélie said nothing. They were sitting on a bench overlooking the Canal Saint-Martin.

"Have you heard anything?" said Madame Strauss. Amélie shook her head. "Nor me. They took my David, caught him in one of those street sweeps. He only went to get some bread."

She sighed. "They came for my husband last year. I was shopping, queued for an hour and a half for cabbage, came home pleased to have enough for both of us, make a nice hot soup I thought. The front door was open. He was gone."

"But not you?" said Amélie. She remembered Madame

Strauss. She was involved with the local synagogue, used to come knocking to try and persuade Papa he should attend more than once in a blue moon. Maman would invite her in for coffee and cake and smile politely before suggesting they agree to disagree. "Live and let live," Maman said in her most sing-songy voice.

"Oh well," Mrs Strauss would say with a dramatic shrug. "I will try again another day."

She seemed a different woman now, but who wasn't? The feeling was gone from her shrugs.

"No, not me," she said. "I have survived... somehow."

They sat in silence for a time, staring at the green surface of the canal. It hardly seemed to move at all.

"I need your help," said Madame Strauss. Amélie said nothing.

"When I saw you it was like my prayers were being answered. Do you pray?"

This time it was Amélie's turn to shrug.

"I have heard, I mean... there were stories that you... that you had..."

"What?"

"Become a, I don't know how to say it...a Resister. You were with the Resistance."

"There are many stories these days."

"I know – she's too young, just a girl I said. How could she survive? But then I thought, there was always something about that girl… I always had you down as a fighter, not like that brother of yours…"

"Don't talk about Paulie like that – you don't know him. You don't know me." Amélie stood up. "I have to go."

"No, please…" Madame Strauss put her hands together, as if she was about to pray there and then. "I'm sorry. I really do need help – there's a home, a children's home." She reached forward and grasped Amélie's left hand. "Children of parents who've been taken…"

"Jewish children?"

"Yes, our children. They are in danger, great danger. The Boche are coming for them. They want to kill every last Jew before they are driven out. We… I mean the woman who runs the home, she has an ally in the city hall – he's seen an order for the home to be closed down. It means they are coming for the children."

"When?"

"Monday, we think Monday afternoon, the train's go in the evening only… we have the weekend, only the weekend to hide them."

Amélie pulled her hand free.

"Will you help us?"

"Yes," said Amélie and placed her hands around Madame Strauss's. One more mission. She felt the certainty of her decision flood through her. She thought of her father, Papa. His face was becoming harder to picture. "It is who I am," he had said. "Yes," thought Amélie. "It is who I am." She had to do this – the Nazis would not have us all.

"Yes, Madame, I will."

* * *

"Absolutely not," said André. "Can't be done. Not by Monday, not in a month of Mondays. There is nothing we can do for them. It's not what we're here for."

Amélie stood up and crossed to the window. She folded her arms and looked out over the rooftops of Paris. From up here it was possible to see across the city, her city, and pretend all was normal. There was no sign of war, no sign of the Germans.

"It's what I'm here for," she said.

"What?" André was still at the table, stirring his spoon in the daily mush – which he refused to admit was even mushier and more tasteless than Amélie's.

In the distance she could see the sun glinting off the Sacré-Coeur. Behind it was her home. She wanted to go home so much it ached.

"You, you British and Americans – you're going to win the war aren't you?"

André nodded. No doubt there.

"No matter what you do here in the weeks before the Americans arrive the war will be won. Then you go home and what will we be left with…"

She turned round to face him.

"What? Freedom? Maybe bread to eat again. Walk the streets when we want, go where we want. Not be scared any more. That's good, that's important – it will be nice not to be scared anymore."

Amélie nodded. She pulled out a chair and sat down opposite him.

"Yes, that will be nice. And school… perhaps I'll go back to school and finish my learning, get my certificate. That would be nice as well – finish my childhood. Maybe I'll have the chance to do that. And I will open my book when the teacher says so and I will concentrate on my fractions and try to forget how he spoke to me when I sat in his class with the Star on my coat and I will look at Madeleine and she will smile at me and I will try to forget how she looked at me when I sat there with the Star on my coat.

"And I will look around the classroom and I will see empty chairs and I will try not to think about classrooms across France with empty chairs and I will try to not look at the teacher and say 'How could you let this happen to us, you and all like you, the Grown-Ups? How?'

"And I will try not to accuse him and all like him and then I will think 'Yes, I did what I could to stop it'. I did what I could to stop the ghosts coming into the classroom, a Star shining on each and every one of their coats. Because I will do what I can, I don't care what you say, you cannot stop me – and I know you won't try.

"I want the Germans gone, oh my goodness I want them gone and I want my Mama and my Papa and my Paulie back – how I long for that and I pray for that even though I don't know who I'm praying to or how I should pray because Mama wasn't bothered about all that. 'We're all people,' she said, 'all different and all the same.'

"All different and all the same… yes, if only the world had listened to Maman, or hugged life like Paulie or been kind like Papa."

Amélie shrugged. "But that's not the way of the grown-up world is it?" She shook her head, answering her own question. "And if we do nothing then 63 children will be taken away on a train on Monday night and when you've gone home there will be 63 more empty chairs in the classrooms of Paris. But that's not what you're here for."

The chair scraped on the wooden floor as she pushed it back and stood up.

"Goodbye, André. I hope you have a good life back home."

She marched out of the room and down the corridor to the apartment's front door.

"Wait." André followed her into the corridor. He still had his spoon in one hand. "Where are you going?"

"Home," said Amélie.

"No," said André, taking a step towards her.

"You can't stop me."

"No," said André, "listen... I don't want to stop you... I want to help you."

Chapter 37

Amélie had to stifle a giggle when she saw them come round the corner and stride along Rue Lamarck.

Madame Strauss led the way, a basket hooked on one arm. The other women, all in their Sunday summer best, which in Paris meant the very best, ready for the picnic outing for the poor children of Rue Lamarck home for waifs and strays. Behind Madame Strauss came Pastor Vergara, taller than the women, bald headed and thin shouldered.

Amélie was waiting across the road from the home. She'd been there with Claudette since before dawn, watching in case the Germans turned up early. Down the alleyway were two of André's men with machine guns in case they did.

It was Madame Strauss who'd suggested the Pastor. He'd given her shelter after her husband was taken. André worked out the numbers – Amélie wasn't very good at numbers, because, as she pointed out, she hadn't finished school. Instead over the weekend she cycled round safe house after safe house, arranging places to hide the children. There were 40 hiding places, which meant 23 had to be taken out of Paris.

"Where?" said André and he and Claudette looked at Amélie. They studied the map. André suggested taking them west towards the Americans. "Non," said Amélie. It was too dangerous, the closer they got to the front the more Germans there were, more checkpoints, and then how would they cross the frontline without being shot at?

"So where?" said André.

Amélie scanned the map. "Yes," she said and banged the table with her fist causing the dirty plates left from breakfast to rattle.

André wasn't coming. That was too much of a risk, not least because if London found out he would be ordered to stop at once. This was not what he was there to do. But the plan was in place and he'd agreed Claudette could help – he could operate the radio for the three days she'd be away… if all went according to plan.

Madame Strauss and her entourage swept up the steps and once the door was opened by a startled looking woman, swept on into the building, Pastor Vergara carried along with them.

Once inside they would act swiftly. The director of the home was a friend of Madame Strauss. She'd told her staff volunteers were coming to take the children on an outing to allow the staff to get the home ready for evacuation. That's what the Germans had informed the director was happening to the children come that afternoon. They were to be taken 'to the east for their own safety.' It fooled nobody.

Soon the first women were emerging, a child's hand gripped tight in each of theirs. Some came out with three children, some even with four. Rigid smiles were fixed on the women's faces. They knew the risk they were taking. The children mostly looked sleepy, some grinned at the excitement of an outing, a couple of the younger ones cried. They would be comforted later, now there was no time.

Madame Strauss came out last, hands full. Amélie, Claudette and the two Resistance fighters followed the procession down the Rue Lamarck, round the corner, over a couple more streets, round another corner and into the open door of l'Oratoire du Louvre, the Pastor's church and home.

By the time Amélie came in – Claudette and the men stayed outside on watch, machine guns concealed in a suitcase – the Pastor and Madame Strauss were seated at a table and the children being shepherded into a queue in front of it. Each child was beckoned forward, given a piece of bread by the Pastor while Madame Strauss checked her list. Tick – this one and two more to rue Saint-Martin, number nine. Tick – this brother and sister and two more to rue Saint-Jacques, number 23. And so it went on.

A woman would come forward and take the children away. Soon 40 were ticked off – every safe house known to André, Amélie and the network was full.

Madame Strauss wrote for a moment longer, folded the papers and handed them to the Pastor. He stood up.

"This list I will bury in the garden, by the apple tree – when the war is over, one of us who survives can recover it. It has the names of each child and where they're hidden – it will help their parents be reunited with them... if they've survived. If not..."

The Pastor shrugged. "Well, it will allow them to be looked after by France."

He looked at Amélie and tore one sheet in half. "The other 23 are yours Mademoiselle – please give this to whoever you leave them with so they too can be found."

Amélie took the paper and pushed it into her pocket. She put her hand out. "Thank you," she said. "You are a brave man, and you, Madame Strauss and all your friends."

Madame Strauss smiled. "If we can't even save the children then…" She made a small shrug. "You take care of yourself, Amélie Dreyfus. I will see you when this is all done, I'll come to the apartment and see your dear Maman, maybe convince her to come to the synagogue after all?"

Amélie could see the tears behind her stiff smile.

"Come," said Madame Strauss, gathering up her four children, "au revoir Amélie and good luck."

* * *

Amélie stared out the window. Luck… good luck. They needed every spare crumb of it. No matter how careful their plan, no matter how ferocious their concentration, all it took was one German checkpoint they hadn't counted on, one search of the train by the men in leather coats, one ticket inspector who smelt a rat and wouldn't look the other way and that was it.

At least she was sure of their plan. Take the small, local trains, pottering from one town to the other – a zig-zag across France: Melun to Sens to Vesoul to Beaune to Chalon-sur-Saône to Bourg and, all being well, the end of the line. The Germans rarely bothered with the locals, especially now they couldn't stop looking west toward the advancing Allies. There was still the police and the possibility of checks at larger stations where they changed trains. And then there was trying to look after six children. She was not a mother, she wasn't even a big sister.

She smiled at the four sitting across the narrow compartment. The youngest was sitting on her lap – Amélie's left leg had gone numb – another next to her. Somewhere else on the train was Claudette with six more, while the two Resistance fighters would follow on the next train with the rest. They would all, if the plan worked, meet up in Annemasse.

The town had leapt off the map when she'd studied it with André and Claudette. Of course! Cécile's whispered words came back to her. She remembered them exactly as Cécile said, heard them in Cécile's voice… "There is one other way out – just in case. Just for you – tell no-one understand, no-one. Annemasse, look on the map, near Geneva, on the border with Switzerland. My brother, Arnaud Tillion, he lives there. He will see you safe."

The train hooted and slowed. Another station. Her stomach tightened. Fear; never far away. She looked around the children. They were young, six, seven, eight, the eldest, a boy, maybe about to turn 10. Did they feel it?

She let her breath out as they pulled into an empty platform. Further down the train a door swung open and a man climbed out. He shoved his hands in his pockets and walked down the platform. Amélie watched him go.

"Are we, miss?"

One of the boys opposite cocked his head to one side as he waited for her answer. He looked like a hungry sparrow waiting to be fed words.

"Oh, pardon… what?"

"Orphanage, miss… are you taking us to an orphanage? That's what my brother says."

"An orphanage? No… no, I'm not taking you to an orphanage. We are going… um, somewhere you can be safe until your mama and papa come home, when the war's finished."

"But they're not coming home, that's what my brother says. He says anybody who goes on the trains doesn't come back again. Everybody knows that, he says. My mama and papa went on the trains a long time ago so that means we're orphans doesn't it?"

He said it matter-of-fact; 'This is the way it is for us.'

Amélie shook her head. "No… no… which is your brother."

He pointed at the older boy, sitting on Amélie's side of the carriage, head nodding gently as he slept.

"Your parents, your mama and papa…" What should

she tell him? She had nothing. Maybe he was telling her something. Maybe she should listen to him. Maybe she was the child here.

She shook her head again. "No, don't give up – what's your name?"

"Lou," he said brightly.

"Lou – your Mama and Papa will always believe in you and you must not give up believing in them. Okay?"

Lou looked puzzled. "So am I an orphan?"

Amélie looked round. His brother was awake. They were all awake, all looking at her waiting for her answer.

She looked at Lou, her face serious, frowning in thought. "I don't have an answer for you. But you do have your brother, and he'll look out for you and you must look out for him. And you have your friends here…" …she waved hand round the compartment… "…and you must look out for them and they look out for you. Your friends can be your family as well, your other family."

Lou narrowed his eyes, head still cocked to one side, considering what she said.

"Okay," he said. "I'm hungry."

Chapter 38

It was night, a chill breeze brushed down the mountains. The children shivered outside the station. Further down the valley lights twinkled.

"Switzerland," said the station master. He was leaning on his broom beneath the archway to the platform, framed by the light behind him. He winked at the children.

"Looks pretty doesn't it? Before the war we used to go over the border whenever we wanted, there's a nice swimming lake just over there, lovely at this time of year when the sun's out." He used his broom to point. "Can't get there now. Barbed wire, guards… people still try, some even get over. There's some desperate people about."

Amélie opened her mouth. *Trust no-one. Trust no-one. Trust…*

"Can you help us, M'sieur?" said Amélie. She had to trust someone. The children were tired, hungry. She had to find Cécile's brother. They'd been lucky so far – no checks at all. Once a gendarme had come through the train, glanced at them and walked on. He wanted nothing to do with a group of children – trouble, that's what they'd be whatever they were up to, too much trouble for a man coming to the end of his shift.

Amélie's right hand was plunged in her pocket, wrapped around a wad of francs. They had no papers for the children, no travel permit for her or Claudette. Instead they had money to wave under noses and hope that made the difference.

She pulled out her hand, letting the station master see what was in it. He looked up at the dark mountains. Then dropped his gaze to the street running away from the station, heading for the town centre.

"We're looking for Arnaud Tillion – do you know him?"

"Tillion? The carpenter?"

"Um, yes. Can you direct us to his house?"

She saw his eyes drop to her hand. "I can pay," she said.

"Non," he said and spun on his heel, moving with a speed that surprised Amélie. He headed into the station, leaving the broom against the wall, and pulled a bunch of keys from his pocket.

"M'sieur," said Amélie, hurrying after him. "Wait… please wait."

He stopped at a blue door and the key rattled in the lock. Amélie caught up with him and held out all the money she had.

"I don't want your money," he said and went into the room without turning on the light. It was warm inside the waiting room, wooden benches ran down three walls, two more benches were back-to-back in the middle, a fireplace glowed at the far end. The man poked at the embers with his boot. Amélie stepped inside.

"We are desperate people, M'sieur."

"I know – bring the children in here. I'll have to lock them in – and no light, in case the patrol comes round. I'll tell you how to get to Tillion's – you come back for the children when you're ready."

"Thank you – there will be some more on the last train…"

The man looked surprised, as if that was too many for his trap. *Trust no-one, trust no-one.* Amélie tried to clear her head. She was tired. What choice did she have? She trusted him.

She left Claudette with the children and followed the station master's directions. The town was quiet. Amélie hurried through the streets, beret pulled low over her eyes.

Arnaud's workshop was easy enough to find – the station master said he lived in the apartment above. Amélie knocked on the door as loudly as she dared. It sounded too loud. She turned round to face the street, expecting to see a German patrol at any second.

"What do you want?"

That voice. Amélie spun round and her mouth dropped open. Her head started to spin.

"No... it can't... you're... you're dead..." she said, putting a hand out to try and steady herself, but instead her legs stopped working altogether. The floor rushed to meet her so she closed her eyes as she fell.

Chapter 39

"Cécile?"

Amélie blinked and sat up. The sun was streaming through the curtain-less window of the small room. She swung her legs off the sofa, the blanket which had covered her coiled on the floor.

Her legs felt wobbly as she crossed to the door, glancing out the window as she did. A bright, clear day. She could see mountains rising above the town.

The door led into a hallway. She could hear voices.

"Cécile?"

She stepped into the kitchen. Two people were sitting at a scarred wooden table. They looked up as Amélie came in.

"Bonjour, my little bird."

Amélie put her hand over her mouth. Cécile stood up.

She'd cut her hair short too, it made her face look sharper. She looked older, tired, but that determination was still there in her face.

Cécile opened her arms and Amélie stepped into them. She stifled a sob into Cécile's shoulder. They stood for a minute, maybe longer, holding each other tight.

"I thought you were…"

Cécile stroked the back of her head.

"I would have been if it hadn't been for you," she said. Amélie looked up. Still they held each other.

"The warning you gave when you got to the coast – that got to me in time. And the fact you threw Raymond off the train!"

Cécile let out a little laugh. They let go of each other and sat down at the table.

"This is my brother, Arnaud…" He nodded a hello, reluctant to interrupt the reunion. He looked a lot like his big sister.

"Raymond held off betraying me and a few others – he wanted to catch as many as possible all at once. He was greedy. What you did gave me time to get away. He still destroyed the network, cost many lives, poor Alain… I still feel guilty."

She shrugged. "I came here. Me and Arnaud, we've been

helping people, Jewish people mainly, cross the border. We've a little network of our own... that's why you have come? You need to get away."

"No, well, yes actually – I mean sort of..."

"Here," said Arnaud, pushing a loaf of bread and a pot of jam across the table. "Eat and tell us."

When she'd finished and licked the last of the jam off her lips, Cécile squeezed her hand.

"It can be done," she said. "We'll need a couple of days but we'll get you across."

"Non," said Amélie. "Not me – I will go back to Paris with Claudette and the men. We're not finished there yet."

Cécile leaned forward and took her other hand as well. "Amélie, ma chérie, it is done, the Germans are losing. Paris will soon be free and then we can go back together."

Amélie pulled her hands away. "I must go back... I must."

"But why?"

"In case..." Amélie put her hands under the table.

"What?"

"Maman and..." Her voice trailed off.

"But..." began Cécile. She hesitated, stood up and began gathering the plates from the table. "Yes," she continued. "I see."

She took the plates over to the sink. "We should make sandwiches for the children. They will be hungry. I'll get more bread."

She turned on the tap, holding a finger beneath it, waiting for the water to heat up. "I understand, Amélie – we'll get you back to Paris. I promise."

Cécile turned to face her and smiled, the smile Amélie remembered so well. "First we have to help you get these children out."

Task one was to collect the children from the station. Arnaud and Cécile saw to that and hurried them down to an old barn on the edge of town that belonged to the Tillion family. Claudette and the men would look after them until it was time to go.

The Germans might be losing the war but they remained determined to show they were masters of the French, determined nobody should escape before the very end.

The usual way to get over the border was under the cover of darkness. Trying to do that with a large group of young children was a non-starter.

Which left daytime, and two risky options. The first was a funeral. The town's cemetery ran right up to the border and instead of barbed wire there was just the head-high cemetery wall. The Germans kept a close eye on anyone entering the cemetery but kept their distance when it came to funerals (after checking there really was a body in the coffin).

So Arnaud and Cécile bribed the local funeral directors – every time there was a burial a handful of the mourners were fugitives. Instead of following the coffin into the church they would dart round to where the gardener had 'accidentally' left his ladder and be over the wall in a flash. The only condition was they left their black armbands and veils at the bottom of the wall to be given back to the funeral director.

But this did not suit a large group of children. Which left one way.

"Football," said Arnaud, bouncing a ball on the hard floor. "That's how we'll do it."

Chapter 40

"Here," said Cécile, "we'll need this."

She handed Amélie a stout walking stick with an odd square cut into the top.

"There's one for Claudette and for your men as well," said Arnaud, who had one arm looped around the football. Amélie knew better than to ask questions. She and the children were in their hands now, as crazy as the escape route seemed.

They collected the children and chivvied them down to the edge of town, crossing a narrow footbridge over the river that led to a small loop of France poking into Switzerland. It was a small park with a football pitch at the bottom of the loop – it was an everyday event to see children kicking a ball around next to the tangle of barbed wire that separated occupied France and neutral Switzerland.

At first the children, wary of new surroundings and the stacked rolls of barbed wire down one touchline, were reluctant to play but with shouts of encouragement from Arnaud they were soon chasing after him and the ball. Shouts and laughs began to replace the still of a Sunday morning. After all that time cooped-up inside the chance to run across grass, sucking in mouthfuls of crystal-clear mountain air brought the Rue Lamarck children alive.

Amélie couldn't help smiling as she watched. Claudette and the two men joined in the game.

"Oh, go away," sighed Cécile. She was looking at a group of German soldiers. They were a little way off, lying on a bank that rose away from the pitch. Jackets undone, caps pushed back on their foreheads, they puffed on cigarettes and enjoyed the sunshine.

"They are supposed to parade on Sunday mornings – in the main square... that gives us the chance to get the kids away before the patrol comes round again."

"How long have we got?"

Cécile glanced at her watch. "A little while yet."

"Careful, Lou," shouted Amélie, seeing the little boy tumble to the ground. He bounced back up again, waved at Amélie and tipped his head back to laugh as he took off again after Arnaud and the ball.

"Come with me – bring the sticks," said Cécile. Amélie gathered the walking sticks Claudette and her men had left on the side of the pitch.

"Shoot, girl, shoot..." Arnaud's cry carried over the children's shouts. A girl, her hair tugged into messy pigtails, kicked hard at the ball and it skipped and bounced through the goalposts.

"Hurray," yelled Arnaud and lifted her up to celebrate. The Germans grinned and clapped. The children flopped down on the grass.

"Keep an eye on the Boche," said Cécile. She took the walking sticks and began to clip them together, the squares carved in the top allowing one to join another. She laid the pole down in the grass where it was out of sight of the Germans and glanced at her watch again.

There was no sign of life on the Swiss side. A grassy slope ran up to a line of trees. A little higher up the hill, Amélie could see rooftops and chimneys poking above the trees.

Either side of the border the trees had been hacked down to make way for the wire and a path for the guards to patrol.

"Come on, come on..." said Cécile. Arnaud joined them. The children were rolling around in the grass, enjoying its softness and the smell of the earth as the sun smiled down on them.

"Perhaps we can distract them," he said.

"How?" wondered Amélie. Arnaud shrugged.

"She's here," said Cécile.

Amélie looked through the wire. A young woman was standing in the cover of the tree line. Next to her a Swiss border guard, rifle slung over his shoulder.

"They will help on the other side – get the children through and away."

The town clock chimed the hour. Arnaud swore under his breath. "The patrol will be here in half an hour, perhaps less," he said.

"Look…" Amélie nodded towards the Germans. They were scrambling to their feet, tugging on jackets, fixing caps in place. They hurried up the bank and out of sight.

"Amélie, go to the top of the bank. It gives a view of the bridge – keep watch. We have maybe 20 minutes before the patrol crosses. Okay?"

Amélie nodded. She hurried over to the children and clapped her hands. Some sat up, others stood up. Lou stood and rubbed his arm. There were grass stains on his shorts.

"Listen, mes enfants – you are to go with Cécile and

Arnaud. You must do as they say. I will see you soon." She blew a kiss at them. "Au revoir."

When she got to the top of the bank she saw the last of the soldiers hurrying over the bridge. She turned and waved at Arnaud. He bent and lifted the pole. On the other side the woman ran forward as he began to slide it through the wire. The Swiss border guard stepped out of the trees and walked a little way along the border. He unslung his rifle.

Amélie swallowed and glanced back at the bridge. All clear. Arnaud and the woman lifted the pole and it lifted a little of the wire, creating enough space for someone to crawl through.

Cécile and Claudette shooed the children towards the wire. Amélie could see Lou hanging back, his brother looking round for him. Amélie looked at her watch. Fifteen minutes. She looked up. Up here in the mountains the sky was bluer than she'd ever seen.

One of her men, she wasn't sure which, began crawling through to show the children what to do. Halfway through he stopped. His sleeve was caught on the wire. He tugged it free and beckoned for the first child to follow him.

Arnaud encouraged the tallest boy forward. It was Lou's brother. He looked back again, put his hand out. Amélie saw Arnaud smile at him and say something. The boy nodded and dropped to his knees. He lay down and began to crawl beneath the wire.

Amélie looked back at the bridge. All clear. Lou's brother was through, behind him snaked a line of wriggling children. Amélie's man helped pull each one out and sent them scurrying for the cover of the trees.

Amélie turned her wrist so she could see her watch. The minute hand was flying round. She swallowed and looked beyond the bridge to the corner of the street where the patrol would first become visible. She turned back and gave the thumbs up to Cécile who waved. She was smiling and that made Amélie smile.

The smile was still on her face as she refocused on the bridge and its approaches. It froze. One, two, three, four, five men, grey tunics, shiny dark helmets, one glinting in the sunshine, rifles… the patrol. She dropped to the ground as if she too were about to crawl under the wire. She twisted her head to look down to the border.

Yes! They were all through. No, wait; Cécile was bent over a small figure. She lay down, patting the ground next to her encouraging the boy to do likewise. It was Lou.

Amélie whistled. Arnaud looked up at the bank. The sight of Amélie flat on her face was the only signal he needed. She could see him urging Cécile and Lou on. Claudette and her other man were looking around. Arnaud said something to them. Cécile sat up and put her arms around Lou. Claudette and the man dropped to the ground and crawled through, a few seconds that was all it took.

Amélie peered over the brow of the bank. The patrol was on the bridge. They'd stopped and were leaning over the railing. One took off his helmet and raised his face to the sun. Another offered cigarettes around. The helmetless one, a sergeant, shook his head and growled an order. There was a murmur of complaint as the others straightened themselves. The helmet was returned to its place, the sergeant hooking the strap over his chin. They crossed the bridge, boots tramping on the wood; trolls on the bridge not beneath it.

Amélie shimmied backwards down the bank. When she thought she was hidden from view she ran, the slope speeding her towards the wire. Her mouth opened as she ran. Arnaud swung round. He had a revolver in his hand. Behind him Lou was tugging at the wire. He was caught. Cécile had gone ahead and coaxed him a little way through. Then he panicked and tried to stand.

Amélie reached the wire. "They're coming," she said. "On the bridge."

"I'll cover you," said Arnaud. He handed her his end of

the pole and ran towards the edge of the bank, where the patrol would emerge on the path besides the wire.

"Arnaud…" Cécile cried. "No…"

There was nothing she could do. Behind her Lou blocked her way back to France. She had to go forward.

"Go," said Amélie. Her chest was heaving, her breathing ragged. "I'll get him."

Cécile slithered on. Amélie dropped to her knees, one arm holding the pole up, and for the first time became aware of Lou's sobs. He was on his knees, torso wrapped in the wire. He had a cut on one leg. There was blood. His woollen sweater, baggy and thin with age, was caught on several barbs.

"Lou…" croaked Amélie. Her mouth was dry. She reached out and managed to get a hold on his left foot. She pulled and he screamed. It startled her, she let go.

"Lou, listen to me…" She stood up, lifting the pole higher, gesturing for the Swiss woman to do the same. It lifted Lou up a little, the sleeves of his sweater stretching. He squealed but it was a cry of fear rather than pain.

"Lou, my darling," said Amélie, trying to find the voice her mother used when she was comforting her. "Can you do something for me… nod if you can, my darling."

A little nod from the back of his head.

"Slide your arms out of your sweater – and slide your head out. Go straight down... wait, wait... and then you can crawl through to Cécile... okay?"

"I want you to come." His voice wobbled.

"Can you do that for me, sweetheart?"

"I want you to come."

"I will, but you must take your sweater off first."

He raised his arms and slid them out, his head followed and he lay down as if he was hugging the ground. He looked back at Amélie.

"Who will hold the pole for you... how will you get through..."

She could hear the panic rising again in his voice. She gave him her best smile. The sweater flapped in the wind. Amélie's smile was shattered by the bark of a shot.

Shouts from beyond the bank. She turned to see Arnaud crouched behind a boulder where the bank angled down to meet the path and the wire. He was peering round the side. She watched as he ducked out fired again and threw himself back behind the boulder.

"Come on..." Cécile waved from the other side. The Swiss guard had his rifle in his hands. Amélie knew he could do nothing to save them – he would not shoot at the Germans.

"Lou – quick, go, go," Amélie barked at the boy. But he wouldn't move.

More shots. This time the crack of rifles. A couple of bullets hit the boulder and whined as they disappeared in different directions. Amélie flinched and ducked. So did the Swiss woman. She dropped the pole.

"You go," shouted Amélie, waving at Cécile. She shook her head.

"Go," repeated Amélie. The Swiss woman and the guard took the second invitation.

"Lou…" she softened her voice as much as she could. Another volley of shots crashed against the rock. Lou moaned.

"You're going to come with me, my darling. Slide backwards… just a little, that's it, good boy…"

He came out backwards and knelt up when he was free of the wire. Amélie dropped the pole and he threw his arms around her waist, tight, pushing the breath from her.

"The woods…" Cécile was pointing. "Get in the woods, follow them, they lead to where the river curves, there are some stepping stones…"

She broke off to glance towards the boulder where her brother was trying to save their lives. Amélie turned to look too. Arnaud leaned out from the boulder and raised his right

306

arm to fire. There was the crack of his pistol; then almost at once the angry cackle of replying rifle fire. Arnaud was knocked back, tumbling to the ground.

"Arnaud!"

He pushed himself back against the boulder one hand clutching his shoulder. He looked down on them.

"Run," he yelled. "Run."

Amélie could see tears in Cécile's eyes. Her voice though was steady. "Cross the river, get through the town, stay off the main streets – get to the station, the station master will help you. Now go…"

"Not until I see you go," said Amélie and offered her friend a last smile. Cécile nodded, turned and ran for the trees.

"Give up or you shot…" One of the patrol was shouting at Arnaud, his bad French delivered in a heavy German accent.

Amélie scooped up Lou. He was skin and bones and that saved both their lives. A normal boy of his age would have been too heavy for a normal girl of Amélie's age to carry.

More shots from the bank. Amélie ran for the treeline. A bullet beat them to it, zipping past and thudding into a tree trunk. She thought she heard a cry from Arnaud as she made the cover of the wood. She didn't turn back.

Chapter 41

Amélie shifted in her seat. Her arm was numb. Lou pressed against her, sleeping, his breath coming in little gasps. He wouldn't let her out of his reach. She closed her eyes. She would have to hide him when they got back to Paris. She knew where.

It was an easy decision. She settled on it as they crouched in the station master's store at the end of the platform in Annemasse, hiding yet again, always hiding. The station master had done just as Cécile suggested, and all without a flicker of emotion except a slight raising of one eyebrow.

He locked them in the store, said he'd let them out when the train came. "Not a sound," he instructed and turned the large key in the lock.

The Germans came later. Amélie felt the boy tense when they heard the first shouts, then the sound of hobnailed boots on the platform. She put her hand across his mouth when the door handle rattled.

"What here is in?" said a German voice in bad French. She couldn't make out the station master's reply but whatever it was the door remained shut and a little while later the platform was quiet again.

It was late afternoon when the door opened. Amélie squinted at the light. "It's coming," said the station master in his one-tone-fits-all voice. "Get in the front carriage – people with something to hide always go in the last one." The corners of his mouth turned down and he shrugged. "The things you learn on the railway.

"The Boche are outside, so you should be okay. They think you'll try for the border again tonight so are not so worried about the station. Be careful – they are angry, two of their men are hurt and they want revenge."

The train puffed tiredly into the station. Everyone was tired, France was tired, tired of war, tired of the Germans, tired of struggling from one day to the next.

The station master opened the carriage door. "I know the conductor – you'll be all right, this goes all the way to Paris."

Amélie thanked him; again a little turn of the mouth, a shrug that said it was nothing. Then she asked the question she didn't want to.

"Arnaud?"

"His sister, the children… they got away. Arnaud…" This time a shake of the station master's head.

They got off the train two stops before the Gare de Lyon – there would be checks there and men in leather coats. Two stops because the leather coats also waited at the next-to-last stop to keep an eye out for people trying to dodge those checks.

It meant a long walk; better tired legs than a stay with the Gestapo on Avenue Foch. She told Lou what the options were when he moaned and when he didn't stop moaning she knelt down to face him, put her hands on his shoulders and looked into his eyes.

"Your brother," she said, "is waiting for you in Switzerland, worrying about you, worrying if you're alive, worrying if you're too little to survive. 'My little Lou cannot beat the Germans, he is only a child'."

She shook her head. "Non… you show him who you are, you show him that it doesn't matter what your age is you – you – can beat the Boche. We will survive, you and me Lou, so that when your brother and my brother come home, we will be here. D'accord?"

She gripped his shoulders tight. Lou sniffed, and after a moment or two nodded.

"D'accord," he said, "I understand."

"Good," said Amélie, standing up and offering him her hand. He took it and they walked on.

"Amélie?"

"Yes."

"Are you going to be my maman?"

"Nooo… of course not. Your maman will be home when the war finishes. I'll look after you until then." She looked down at him. "Besides I'm too young to be your maman – your big sister maybe, your just-for-the-moment big sister."

"How old are you, Amélie?" His voice was brightening, his spirit returning.

"I'm… I'm…" How old? Amélie shook her head. How old was she? By her ID card she was 18, as good as grown-up. But she wasn't 18.

"How old, Amélie?"

She didn't know, not right away. The thought slapped her in the face hard enough to make her stop.

"Can't you count? I can, I'm six, seven next birthday."

She'd been pretending for so long so she didn't know unless she worked it out.

"Come on," she said, quickening her step, "we need to get home."

"Where's home?"

"You'll see – it's a surprise."

Home. She still knew where that was. Amélie put her hand to her throat and felt the two necklaces, she pulled them both up and closed her hand around the key and the moon.

They stopped at a café to eat and Amélie asked to use the telephone. André answered.

It was another long walk to the cemetery and they were both tired by the time they stood and waited beneath the lion tamer. Lou enjoyed the story of the lion eating the lion tamer. André took them to a safe house for the night and in the morning she told him she was going home.

She took off the necklace with the crescent moon and handed it to him. "When you go home," she said, "give this to Vera with my love."

André shut his fist around the necklace. She could see he was considering his next move. But what choice did he have? No Claudette, two of his men gone and now Amélie…

Head bowed, he nodded slowly and put the necklace in his pocket. He looked up and smiled.

"Very well – I have one condition…"

Amélie steeled herself. She was determined to say no…

"If you're ever in London promise you'll look me up –

telephone Chiswick 789. Girl like you will have no problem remembering that eh?"

Amélie nodded. He put out a hand and patted her on the shoulder.

"Au revoir," he said.

"So long, André." She opened the door, ushered Lou into the street and closed it behind her.

Chapter 42

It was like a scene from a fairy tale where time had frozen. Nothing had changed inside. Everything had changed outside. The sign on the front of the apartment block, 'No Jews', had gone. There was a dirty mark on the wall where it had been, a stain too where Vette's paint had been scrubbed off.

"Is this our new home?" wondered Lou as he followed Amélie down the hallway.

She turned into the living room. It smelt funny, musty, lifeless. A thick layer of dust covered everything. Amélie opened the big window – it stuck halfway up. Lou sneezed.

"Is it?" he said, sniffed and wiped his nose on his sleeve.

"Come," said Amélie and led him into the bathroom.

She remembered the tub being larger. "I'm not having a bath," said Lou retreating into the corridor.

Amélie knelt and used her sleeve to brush away some of the dust on the floor. She dug her fingers beneath the loose floorboard and lifted it clear. The suitcase was where she'd left it.

She took out the fur coat and Champs-Élysées and pressed both to her face. Their smell was gone.

"Will this be my room?" She followed Lou's shout and found him in her room.

"Perhaps," she said. "Come – I need to show you something important."

They went into her parents' room. She opened the wardrobe door and hung the fur coat back in its place. She stepped inside.

"Come," she said beckoning Lou. She pushed back against the other clothes hanging in the wardrobe, allowing Lou to squeeze in beside her.

"There," she said and pulled the fur coat aside to reveal her ledge. "You get on there."

Lou scrambled on and she closed the door. It gave a familiar click.

"It's dark," said Lou. "Amélie... it's dark."

"We're safe here," she said, pushing her hand past the

coat, finding his and squeezing it. "If anyone comes this is where you hide, close the door and stay on the ledge. Understand?"

She squeezed his hand, harder than she should. "Oww," he said.

"Understand?"

"Like cache-cache…"

"Yes," said Amélie, an unseen smile forming on her face in the darkness, "like hide and seek."

It became his favourite game. They played in between Amélie scrubbing the apartment from top to bottom. She was determined it would be spotless for her family's return. Lou wasn't very good at hiding so Amélie had to pretend to search for a time before opening the wardrobe, pulling back the fur coat to discover him crouched on her ledge. It was the only place he ever hid.

"Ta-daaah," he would say and leap out.

She didn't let him outside the apartment, locking him in when she went out to find what food she could.

The Germans were going. Trucks loaded with loot by soldiers with angry faces. Amélie kept her gaze on the ground and hurried past.

One morning the sound of shots carried through the apartment's open windows – the musty smell was just about gone – and Amélie hurried Lou into the wardrobe. Later that day a lorry packed with armed men drove past. It was flying the French flag. She thought she caught sight of André among them.

Two days later and the Germans were gone. Amélie took Lou and they wandered the streets, along with hundreds of others, as if in a daze. Was it really true? Were they gone? For good?

They turned a corner. The crowds thickened. There was a vehicle, an armoured car with the red, white and blue lines of the flag of France fluttering from its turret, coming slowly down the street, a bearded man, a captain, in its turret. It stopped near Amélie and Lou – there were too many people packing the road for it to go any further. The captain climbed on to the front of the armoured car and waved at the crowds to make way. Instead two women clambered on to the armoured car and embraced him.

Someone began a song – the Marseillaise, the anthem of France. The bearded captain reappeared, now carried on the shoulders of two men. He had a splodge of lipstick on his forehead, and he was crying. He raised a fist into the air and yelled. "Vive la France! Vive la France!"

Everyone joined in, Amélie, holding tight to Lou's hand, raised her other hand and yelled with him and then they were all singing and Amélie felt the tears well in her eyes.

"It's over," she said, hugging Lou to her, "it's really over."

Except it wasn't.

Two days later there was a victory parade along the Champs-Élysées. Amélie took Lou because he wanted to see French tanks and French soldiers, to see they really existed. Amélie didn't want to go, she didn't want to leave the apartment in case they came home.

The streets were busy, full of smiles and full of people claiming to have been in the Resistance, men, all men, with red, white and blue armbands strutting around.

"Pah," said a woman standing next to them. "Those Ice Creams better not spend too long in the sun. They melted away in 1940 and now look at them…"

Amélie didn't recognise any of them.

"My Amélie is in the Resistance, aren't you Amélie?" Lou tugged at her arm.

The woman looked her up and down. "Really? You don't look old enough, my dear."

"It doesn't matter," said Amélie.

She took Lou home, climbing the narrow streets to Montmartre and curling up together in Maman and Papa's bed, the comforting outline of the wardrobe visible in the blurred light of a summer night.

France may have been freed but the war was not yet done. Germany fought on. Paris tried to get on with life, Amélie tried but it was hard. Then the British, Americans and Russians found the camps and the very worst of the stories turned out to be all too true; concentration camps where Jewish people had been taken and terrible, terrible things done to them, men, women and children. Children of all ages, like the ones Amélie helped escape, like Lou, herded into gas chambers never to see the light of day again, some clutching their mother's hand as they died, others alone, lost, terrified. So many dead, so few alive.

Amélie shook her head and got on with making the apartment cleaner than it had ever been. They would come back, they would come back. She scrubbed and scrubbed until it shone.

There was an office set up for missing persons in the Hotel Lutetia on the boulevard Raspail. Amélie packed Lou off to school and became a regular at the Lutetia, pestering them for information. It was there she saw Vera. The Englishwoman was trying to trace missing agents.

"I was hoping I might bump into you," said Vera, making

Amélie wonder how much of a coincidence their meeting was.

"I want you to have this back," said Vera and handed over the crescent moon necklace. There was another pendant attached to the chain, a small silver star. "And I want to help you."

They had lunch at the Ritz – much better than the English version – and Vera offered Amélie a job, assisting her in the search for the agents. It meant Amélie could be at the Hotel Lutetia every day, and it also meant she could earn money to look after her and Lou. They found Cécile, she was safe and back in Annemasse. There was still no trace of Lou's brother. So many missing.

And then Germany surrendered. The war really was over.

Chapter 43

They began coming back from the camps. Amélie cried when she saw the first survivors limp off the train, bent but trying not to be broken. She walked among them asking 'Dreyfus, Dreyfus, do you know Dreyfus?' There was no answer, just the shuffling of feet along the platform.

She badgered officials at the Hotel Lutetia. They had nothing for her. Vera discovered the fate of her missing agents. They wouldn't be coming home. Her work was done. She hugged Amélie and went back to London, having promised to keep paying her for as long as she could get away with it. Six months at most, Vera thought.

"Britain, and France, they want to forget about the war – move on," said Vera.

"I will wait," said Amélie, her jaw set stubborn, a look Vera had come to know well.

And then, at last, news. An autumn day, sunny but with that first breath of cold.

"We have been sent a final list from Germany," said Claude, a young man in the office – a smaller office now in a smaller building. "It's those who will not be on the trains… what I mean is names of those who will not be coming home…"

He was ex-Resistance too. She liked him, he was kind to her. He looked down at the list, couldn't look at her.

"Their names… their names are on it. A Dreyfus, male, S Dreyfus, female."

Amélie sat down on the chair in front of his desk. Maman. Papa. She looked at her hands, resting in her lap. She wished she could have been hugged one last time. Maman. Papa.

"I'm sorry, Amélie, truly I am," said Claude. He came round from his desk and hovered beside her, unsure what to do.

Amélie wanted to cry. She wanted to curl up and cry, shut herself in the wardrobe and wrap Maman's fur coat tight around her. She sniffed. She wouldn't cry here. She would wait until she got home.

She stood up and nodded at Claude. "Thank you," she said, hurried out of the room and down the stairs. Halfway down she stopped. A Dreyfus, Albert Dreyfus, and S

Dreyfus, Sarah Dreyfus. No P Dreyfus. Paulie? What about Paulie?

She climbed back up the stairs, opened the office door without knocking. Claude looked up.

"Paulie – what about my brother?"

Claude ran his finger down the list of names one more time. It took a while. "There's no other Dreyfus here. Wait… give me a minute."

He left the room. She crossed to the window, trying to find something to look at. Her eyes were cloudy. "No loose ends, Maman," she whispered. One minute, two, several more. Claude returned.

"There is nothing, no record of him."

Amélie's head dropped, she tried not to let it but couldn't keep it up. Not anymore.

"There is one possibility… I shouldn't be telling you this because his name's not on the list. There's a last train coming – will be here in…" he looked at his watch… "under an hour. These are the last known French survivors of the camps. I don't think he's on it but sometimes… sometimes there can be mistakes, people can be missed…"

His voice trailed off. He shrugged. "I don't want to give you false hope…"

"Thank you," said Amélie.

She took a taxi to Gare Montparnasse. The streets were busy. Parisians had their cars back and were determined to use them as much as possible.

"Please," she said, leaning forward to the driver. "As quickly as possible."

He did his best but the train had already pulled into the station by the time she made the platform. It was busy. Nurses were helping the freed prisoners from the carriages. Relatives, desperate for a first glance of loved ones, pushed and shoved each other – taking care not to touch the prisoners in case they might break.

Amélie stood on her tip-toes and peered along the platform. It was no use. The prisoners looked alike, dressed in the same loose smocks and trousers given them when they'd been released. Their appearance no longer shocked her; shaved heads, skeleton thin, all not quite able to believe they were alive, that they were in Paris.

The crowds thinned. Amélie walked a little way along the platform. A man ever so slowly climbed out of the nearest carriage. She spun to face him. He looked the oldest man she'd ever seen.

"Typical," he said, his voice croaky. "Fall asleep at the moment I've been dreaming of for three years, two months and 17 days. Or is it 18… I forget…"

He shrugged, smiled at her and began a slow, hunched walk down the platform. There was a shriek from the barrier and a woman ran towards him, tears tumbling down her cheeks. Amélie sniffed. She was struggling now, tears pressed against her eyes, demanding to come out.

"Amélie?"

She froze. The voice was behind her. She didn't want to turn around, she didn't dare turn around. What if… what if it wasn't…

"Is… is that you, Amélie?"

She turned around. "Paulie."

"Found you," he said and opened his arms.

FIN

Notes & Acknowledgements

"The world doesn't feel so frightening when you're young."
Stephen Grady, 16-year-old French Resistance member
Gardens of Stone

Amélie Dreyfus is, of course, a fictional character but I built her experiences during the Second World War from reading a number of history books and memoirs about the occupation of France. Children did play a part in the French Resistance, and in resistance groups right across Europe from Holland, France and Belgium to Poland, Ukraine and Russia.

Stephen Grady was a schoolboy resistance fighter, the son of a French mother and British father. He was just a teenager when he risked his life alongside adults in the north of France. "The less you know," he wrote in *Gardens of Stone*, "the braver you can be." I highly recommend his book – it tells the extraordinary tale of an exceptionally courageous boy.

Maurice Buckmaster, who is Amelie's boss in my story, was head of the French Section of the Special Operations Executive, a curious name for a British spy and sabotage group. The SOE had a decidedly mixed record in France, making many mistakes that were often fatal for their agents. Among them some remarkable women like Noor Inayat Khan and Violette Szabo, were captured, tortured and executed in concentration camps. If you want to find out more about Noor Inayat Khan's story, try Sufiya Ahmed's *My Story* published last year. The youngest agent to land in France was Sonya Butt. She was 19 when she joined SOE and survived the war.

Buckmaster wrote *They Fought Alone* about his wartime experiences; a fascinating read full of small details about preparing the agents. They really did have boxes of earth from different parts of France in a flat in London with a black-tiled bathroom. Vera Atkins worked with Buckmaster looking after the female agents.

Excellent books on the French Resistance by Richard Vinen, *The Unfree French*, and Robert Gildea, *Fighters in the Shadows*, are well worth a look as is Caroline Moorhead's *Village of Secrets* which tells the story of a number of villages on the Vivarais-Lignon Plateau in the Massif Central that sheltered those facing Nazi persecution, including thousands of Jewish people, many of them children.

Two black-and-white photographs played a significant part in inspiring the story of Amélie Dreyfus. The first is of Simone Segouin, said to be 18 when the picture was taken. In the photograph she looks younger – little older than my 13-year-old daughter. She's dressed as you might expect a teenage girl in a 1940s Paris summer to be, a patterned blouse, neat pair of shorts and white socks. And she holds a German machine gun, ready for use, a military cap on her head. The contrast is striking. It's a picture you can't take your eyes from… you have to know more.

The photo was taken during the liberation of Paris in 1944 – Simone was a resistance fighter (who is still alive). She'd been involved in the resistance since she was 17.

The other photo is, by contrast, one a parent or grandparent might have on the mantlepiece. A studio photo, it's of Eva Redischova, with her bobbed haircut and large eyes. She was born in Prague in 1931 and murdered in a gas chamber in Auschwitz 13 years later. The photo appeared on the Twitter feed of the Auschwitz Museum (@AuschwitzMuseum – please follow them. Eva's is a picture that haunts you, its ordinariness concealing a story of utter tragedy.

I wanted Amélie to be a fighter, as much by accident as design as that is true of most of the children who took part in the resistance. I wanted her to be a reflection of the many Jewish resistance fighters from across Europe whose stories have not been widely told in this country.

Like Hannah Szenes, a 23-year-old Jewish Hungarian poet and SOE agent executed in 1944. "A voice called, and I went. I went, for a voice called," she wrote in her cell awaiting her fate. Do look up her story. From Simone to Eva to Hannah, these are people we must always remember and whose stories we should always be telling.

There are so many people to thank for their help in making this book. First up, Mikka, my editor and publisher at Everything With Words. I am blessed to have her encouragement, enthusiasm (for this book and children's books in general), guidance, belief and razor-sharp editorial skill and judgement. Thank you for everything Mikka.

This is the third cover Holly has designed for a book I've written and each one has captured the story better than I could have wished for. Do have a look at her website (www.hollyovenden.com) to see the true range of her amazing talent. A huge thank you to Fritha for her advice, knowledge and for getting the story out there – she is such a great and persistent champion of children's books across the board.

Thank you to Fred for taking an early look at the story's opening chapters and giving it the thumbs up. I'm fortunate to have the support of brilliant friends both in Helensburgh and further afield, none more so than Tony and John, who from the start have been enthusiastic, encouraging and given plenty of advice over several pints, curries and glasses of Gavi di Gavi.

Iona and Torrin are why I write – thank you girls. And none of this would happen without Karen, reader, cajoler, adviser, encourager and above all partner. I will always owe her.

Robin Scott-Elliot has been a sports journalist for 25 years with the BBC, ITV, Sunday Times, Independent and the 'i', covering every sport you can think of and a few you probably can't. In 2012 he covered the London Paralympics as the Independent's Paralympic Correspondent. He threw that all away to move home to Scotland and write. He lives on the west coast with his wife and two children.